Copyright page

Raven's Hart

Haven Hart book 7

Copyright © 2019 by Davidson King

Website: www.davidsonking.com

ALL RIGHTS RESERVED

Interior design and cover design by Designs by Morningstar

Editing done by Steph Carrano

Proofreading provided by Anita Ford

Interior Design and Formatting provided by Flawless Touch Formatting

The unauthorized reproduction or distribution of this copyrighted work is illegal. No part of this book may be reproduced or transmitted in any form or by any means, including electronic or mechanical means, including photocopying, recording, or by any information storage and retrieval systems, without express written permission from the author, Davidson King. The only exception is in the case of brief quotations embodied in reviews.

This book is a work of fiction. While references may be made to actual places and events, the names, characters, places, and incidents either are products of the author's imagination or are used fictitiously. Any resemblance to actual persons, living or dead, events, or locales is entirely coincidental.

Licensed material is being used for illustrative purposes only and any person depicted in the licensed material is a model.

Trademarks

No part of this publication may be reproduced, stored in a retrieval system, or transmitted, in any form or in any means – by electronic, mechanical, photocopying, recording or otherwise – without prior written permission, except in the case of the brief quotations embodied in the critical reviews and certain other noncommercial uses permitted by copyright law. Please purchase only authorized electronic or print editions and do not participate in or encourage the electronic piracy of copyrighted material. Your support of the author's rights is appreciated. This book is a work of fiction. Names, characters, places, and incidents are a product of the author's imagination or are used fictitiously. Any resemblance to actual events, locales, or persons, living or dead, is coincidental. All products and/or brand names mentioned are registered trademarks of their respective holders/companies.

Warnings

This book contains strong sexual content, violence, and language and is not suitable for people under the age of 18.

Dedication

This book is dedicated to my mother Patricia. Through this entire series she has cheered me on, read every book, and been a huge support. I love you, mom. Thanks for always believing in me.

Prologue

1999
Poe

The last few days had been strange but today, July 22, 1999, was by far the strangest and most unforgettable. It was the day He spoke to me for the very first time.

My mother and father were in the clubhouse with the rest of the Hart family's staff watching television. It had been that way every day since the announcement that JFK Jr's plane had crashed. Today they found the bodies and no one left their televisions, perhaps hoping it wasn't them at all.

I was spending the hot summer day doing what I did pretty much every day. Drawing. There was a wonderful weeping willow tree that cascaded over an oak bench along the glistening pond in the Hart's backyard. The shade it provided was perfect for me.

I always knew I was different, and my mother often told me my life wouldn't be easy. At ten years old, I had to wear thick black glasses and avoid the light if I didn't want raging headaches. It was explained to me I had achromatopsia. In short, they told me I could only see in black and white and shades of gray. Light was not my friend and to be a good boy and listen to the doctors.

Being unable to play in the sun like the other kids often had me enjoying my own company. The Harts weren't mean to me, they mostly just ignored me. That, coupled with the fact there wasn't anyone who wanted to play with me, brought me to this very spot where I found peace. But on this day in July, I became some awful kids' entertainment. But not for long.

"Look, Evan, it's the vampire," one boy, who was stocky and had freckles, said with a chuckle.

"Be careful, Jimmy, if you get too close, he'll bite you," the other boy, I assumed was Evan, responded.

"Should you be out in this, freak? You might combust." Both cackled at their unoriginal comment. I just went on drawing and ignored them.

"Shit, you deaf too?" I wasn't looking at them now, so I didn't know which spoke, but a second later, I felt something hit my leg. A rock. They threw a rock at me.

"I'm not a vampire, nor am I target practice. Just go back and find Mas—" Another rock hit, this time at my side making me flinch.

"Oh no, Jimmy, he's gonna charge us." Evan's tone was dripping with sarcasm, and if I didn't want to get seriously injured, I'd have to abandon my favorite spot.

As quickly as possible, I gathered my sketch pad and pencils and began walking the other way. Another rock hit me in the back, and my feet tangled together. My sketch pad went flying as did my pencils.

"Careful, vampire, you don't want one of those pencils stabbing your heart." I believed that was Jimmy's voice. I was getting better at identifying them without looking.

If I didn't get back inside, I was surely going to start bleeding. Being bullied wasn't a new thing for me. When I'd lived in Russia with my parents, I remember being teased because they'd dress me in long coats and dark glasses; while I'd liked it, it was forever weird to others. At six, that wasn't easy to deal with, but the fact it was adults being cruel was shitty. At least they didn't throw things at me like Thing One and Thing Two here.

I'd just gathered my things and was rushing toward the house when I heard his voice. He was two years younger than me, but he was big. I could tell his hair was light in color—my mom said it was blond when I asked. I didn't know the shade of his eyes, but they glittered like the pond. Whenever I looked at Phineas Hart, the air left my body for the briefest of moments.

"What do you two morons think you're doing?" He was racing toward us, anger showed in his beautiful features. Evan and Jimmy weren't laughing anymore, and when I peered over my shoulder, I'd say they seemed terrified.

"We were looking for you," Jimmy said with a shrug, trying to play off his obvious nervousness.

"Is that right?" Phineas said as he stood next to me. For the briefest moment, I thought he was going to lay into me, too, but through my thick glasses, I saw the hint of a smile. It was as warm as the summer sun and I was no longer afraid.

"Yeah," Evan said as he toed the grass.

"Well, here I am." He held his arms out. He didn't look like he was eight, he looked more like eighteen. His presence was powerful. Like all the Harts, it was like he was touched by God himself. He was taller than Evan and Jimmy, not taller than me, but he was two years younger and I had my father's genes, so I knew I'd be close to six feet when I grew up, maybe bigger.

"'Kay, so wanna see the Pokémon cards I got today?" Evan took out some cards from his back pocket and approached Phineas. He held them out and just as he was about to say something more, Phineas smacked them to the ground.

"I don't want you coming by here anymore, Evan. You neither, Jimmy. Poe lives here at this house and if you're gonna be jerks, then you can't come by. Take your stupid cards and get out of here." He didn't yell because he didn't have to. His hands were clenched, and his eyes narrowed in obvious rage... for me.

"Seriously, Phin? But he's so weird," Jimmy said, and immediately took three steps back as Phineas took three steps forward.

"You best be leaving, Jimmy, before I ask my father to make the bad people go away. I said you aren't welcome here anymore, so either get outta here or I'm going to scream." He cocked his head to the side. "How many people you think will come running when they hear me yell for help?"

Evan was halfway down the lawn before Jimmy tuned into what was happening. Once the two of them were out of sight, Phineas turned to me.

"Sorry about that, Poe. They're jerks and won't be coming here anymore." His smile was almost too bright for my eyes.

"Oh, um, it's okay, Master Hart. I…" He cut me off with a laugh.

"God, please don't ever call me that again. Just Phin."

I nodded but felt like I shouldn't be in his presence. My parents told me once they were hired by the Hart family to run the household that I was to stay out of sight. I was homeschooled here, and my best friend was a boy who tended the horses with his father. I rarely saw him, so it was just me and my shadow.

"Wanna play?" Phin asked, and I felt my eyes widen. No way he could see the shock through the darkness of my glasses, but it was there.

"Play?" I looked around wondering if maybe someone else was behind me.

"Yes, it's what kids do. We're kids." He swiped his finger from me to him. "We can swim in the pond, or watch a movie, or I dunno, anything."

"You want to play with me?"

He chuckled. "'Course I do, Poe. Come on. You've been here like a year and I never see you. Finally, I got up the nerve to ask you to play."

Got up the nerve? He was afraid of me? "Why do you call me Poe?" I asked finally, wondering.

His brows shot to his hairline. "Well, I dunno. I heard your name was Raven but I saw on the papers, when I snuck into my parents' room, that your middle name was Poe. My tutor forced me to read 'The Raven' by Edgar Allan Poe. Didn't understand, like, any of it." Phineas shrugged. "I mean I'm eight, what was she thinking? Anyway, it was kinda creepy and whatever. I liked the name Poe, though, and I thought Poe was more you. So, yeah, I can call you Raven if you want."

Suddenly, I didn't want that. I loved that he saw me differently, and I wanted to be called Poe more than anything.

"I like it, thanks."

He smiled again. "So you call me Phin and I call you Poe. P and P."

I laughed then. "Just not peepee." Now we were both laughing hysterically.

"Yeah, that's not good. Come on. Let's go inside where it's cooler and watch a movie. My dad got *The Blair Witch Project*. Looks scary, wanna see it?"

I wasn't sure I did. Movies were sometimes hard to see, but Phineas Hart wanted to hang out with me and I wasn't saying no.

"Sure. Didn't that only just hit the theaters the other day?"

He nodded as we walked back toward the house. Well, castle really. It was massive and had towers and everything.

"Yeah, but when my dad wants something, he usually gets it." He shrugged like that wasn't a scary thing to hear. The Harts ran all of Haven Hart. I didn't understand exactly what they did, but my mom told me they made sure everything ran smoothly. They weren't flashy and often avoided the limelight. Dad said it was for safety reasons. I couldn't understand not wanting to venture out and see all the good they were doing. At least I assumed it was all good.

"I see," I said as we stepped inside. The cool air slammed into me and relief washed over my body.

"Theater room is this way."

I followed him through the long hallways and down several

flights of stairs. I'd never been on this side of the house before and was excited and nervous. What a wonderful feeling.

"Jana, can you pop us some popcorn, please?" he asked one of the staff. I knew Jana. She was from England and started around the same time my parents did.

"Surely, Master Hart." She winked at me as she passed, and I wondered what my parents were going to say to me later when they found out.

The seats in the theater room were like clouds. It was dark, quiet, and comfortable. The perfect room for someone like me.

"I can adjust the brightness on the screen if you want. I know light bothers you, and I want you to see some of it. A lot of it's dark, though, I'm told." He was pushing back a velvet curtain exposing a huge screen. "I don't know much about you, Poe." He turned and smiled again. "Can't wait to find out, though."

Phin was like sunlight and warmth. I'd seen him all over the place, even if he never saw me. He was always laughing, and I suddenly wanted to know everything about him, too.

"I can't wait to find out all about you, too," I answered, earning me an even bigger smile.

That summer was the best I ever had. And the years I was with Phin in that house growing up were everything to me. It was us against the world he'd always tell me when one of us was upset. He'd try and make me feel better, and I'd do my best to make him feel better.

I learned so much about Phin the boy and grew to love Phin the man. And then, as suddenly as he stormed into my life, he was gone, and I was left with a life I never thought I'd have.

Chapter One

Poe

"Why do the leaves on the weeping willow tree look like the faces of the dead?"

I had a private studio on Fifth Avenue above the Out of Focus Gallery. I used to be here more often, but my life only allowed me a few hours in the early morning of every Thursday to indulge in one of my passions. Life had been so crazy lately, that even the Thursdays had become fewer and fewer. Today I wanted to paint, but as I was walking into my studio, I ran into Quill.

While I cared greatly for him, I really wanted to be alone. When I stated that fact, he pouted. He did the whole batting of the eyes and everything. He promised to be quiet, but I guessed that was just wishful thinking.

"First of all, Quill, the leaves on a weeping willow are far too thin to paint crisp individual faces. What I've done is add a facial feature to each leaf, and as they move and connect, a face appears." I dipped my brush into the paint, and the second it hit canvas, he spoke again.

"But why are they dead faces?"

"They aren't dead and—" It was no use. I placed the brush down and turned to face the inquisitive person who'd won Black's heart. How those two made it work was beyond my understanding. Quill was once a barista working his way through life, in and out of horrible relationships. Black owned an assassin organization and was rich beyond necessary means. They were like apples and oranges, but they worked.

"I'm bothering you. I'm sorry." He imitated zipping his lips, but the moment was gone. I couldn't paint with him watching over my shoulder.

"I doubt you bumped into me on the street by accident, or that you want to sit here and watch me paint. Why don't we pretend we had a genius back and forth and I coaxed it out of you? What is it you want?" I folded my legs and waited patiently.

I knew there was an ulterior motive to this meet-up. While my studio was above the gallery, it wasn't the area people bumped into others. The coffee shop was the opposite way, and the only other thing near here was a glass shop and a jeweler. Two places I would bet money Quill wasn't going to.

"I want to start this off with saying I didn't want to be the one to come here. But Teddy made us draw straws, and I grabbed the small one. I tried to trade it, but no one was budging." He was speaking a mile a minute, and it reminded me of a child. Luckily, I spoke child, so I followed him with ease.

"I didn't realize speaking with me was such a chore. So, get on with it, and I'll let you be free of your burden."

Quill's smile dropped and his happiness was replaced with regret and sadness. "No, you don't understand. If it was me inviting you to a thing, it would be easy. Or, like, if I wanted a picture of dead-faced trees, I'd be here voluntarily." He pointed to my painting, and I was resigned to throwing it away as soon as he left.

"Then why are you here?"

He sat down on the floor, paying no mind to the three other chairs in the room. "We didn't see you after Bryce's funeral, and Snow said you sort of talked to him, and then you stopped going to meditation completely. So then I was in my living room one night, and I heard Black on the phone and he mentioned a thing. I was not loving not knowing this thing, so I asked him."

"This is going to take a while, so it seems. I'm getting myself some tea, want some?" I stood and made my way over to the small kitchen.

"Nah, I'm good. So anyway." He spoke louder, seeming to think I couldn't hear him from three extra feet away. "This thing had me thinking, and so I was at the park with Teddy, Snow, and Xander, right?"

"If you say so." With the kettle getting warm, I leaned against the counter and listened.

"Who's Adelaide?" He blurted it out so suddenly I had no time to hide my reaction. "Someone important then." He nodded. "I get it. But with all the shit that happened with Ginger, Lee, and Jones, with Joey and the human trafficking ring, how did this Adelaide become a part of it and who are they to you?"

The kettle began to whistle, glad for the distraction, I quietly fixed my tea.

"Poe."

"Quill. Stop."

Tea in hand I went back to my seat. "Go back to your friends and tell them you followed through on your mission. Tell them you got nowhere." The swirls of steam were mesmerizing, so I kept my focus on them. "You can't barter for the right to invade my privacy."

Quill slammed his hands against the floor and jumped up. The sudden movement had me jerking back. I wasn't afraid of Quill but his sudden spark of anger was unusual.

"You don't make being your friend very easy, Poe. I can't knock on your door and say, *let's go out and do something*. You give off this vibe, this fuck off vibe. You didn't used to be this way. It's gotten…"

"Gotten what?" I had to know how he saw me, how they were all seeing me. I knew my life was jolting out of control. My once steady hold was slipping.

"Impossible to talk to you. We miss you."

Missed me? "How, I'm right here." The bubbling rage I thought wasn't going to arise today made itself known. "But you all only contact me when there's a problem you need fixing." Rising from the chair, I placed my tea on the stool beside my easel. "When was the last time you, or anyone else, tried to knock on my door and ask me if I wanted to go out?"

Quill smirked, but his narrowing eyes belied his happiness. "And where do you fucking live that we can knock on your door, Poe?"

Well, shit. "You're here, aren't you?" I knew that wasn't going to cut it.

"You don't live here. I had to sit on a bench and wait here hoping you'd show today. Every day for the last week I've sat there." That solidified that he didn't just bump into me.

I knew Quill's inquiry about Adelaide wasn't malicious. I knew he'd keep it a secret if I asked, but I'd gotten so used to sharing nothing. Keeping that part of my life sealed like the vaults. Away from those who could hurt her... them.

"If I asked you to give me a little more time, would you respect that answer?"

His rigid stance relaxed and he nodded. "Yeah, okay."

"Thank you."

Chapter Two

Poe

The ride home was long, and I wasn't always able to make it there every night. Who was I kidding? Sometimes it was weeks. I'd stay at the studio many nights because the drive home was so out of the way, and oftentimes, I wasn't done working until late. After the death of my former assistant, Bryce, and the madness that ensued thereafter, I was only able to return home in short stints. Unfortunately, after a disaster, there was cleanup and I had been stuck in Haven Hart longer than usual this time and I missed home.

Due to my condition, I wasn't allowed to drive. They didn't give out licenses that only allowed night driving, so I was driven everywhere or I often walked, which when the sun wasn't out full force, I loved it. I was tall, close to six feet. I wasn't muscular, but I made sure to stay fit with swimming and weightlifting. I had only one driver and I'd known him since I was nine. Corey helped his father with the horses on the Hart estate for years. When the time came, I needed to surround myself with people I trusted to protect what I held dear. Corey came through for me.

The only reason he knew so much was because he experienced so much of it with me. Long before I met Snow, Teddy, Quill, or the others, Corey was there. A quiet presence.

"Almost home," Corey said, and the fluttering warmth I always felt in my chest bubbled. I put away my work and watched out the window as the place I called home appeared.

It was autumn, and while I knew many people loved it for the bright colors, I loved the crisp air. I loved to stand on my balcony at dusk and either paint or play one of my instruments. I adored the smells that brought the promise of bonfires and trick or treaters. I loved that in three days it would be Adelaide's birthday and I'd be there to celebrate.

"So, you're staying here for a while this time?" Corey asked, and I knew he wondered if he'd be able to take a break. I dragged him everywhere.

"Yes, ten glorious days. Go home to your beautiful wife and kids, Corey. I'll call if I need you."

I didn't live in Haven Hart. I was a good two hours away from it at a location only a few people knew of. Corey and his family lived ten minutes from me in a house I'd built for them. I had a housekeeper, a gardener, five security people, a nurse, and a doctor who visited often. Each person that was on this estate I'd known for years. They were the keepers of my secrets. The shields against the outside world. They were vital to the safety of those I loved most in the world.

"Thanks. I got Stephanie that Roomba she wanted, and the kids and I are putting googly eyes on it." He chuckled, and the tug on my lips reminded me how little I smiled these days.

"Enjoy your time. I expect a quiet week."

Once the car was parked in the large garage, I stepped out and waved at Corey as he made his way to his car, eager to get home.

"Welcome home, sir," Tony, my head of security, greeted me as I came to the door.

"Thanks, Tony. For the billionth time, please don't call me sir. I get enough of that day to day, I've known you for years. Poe is my name. I want this place to be as far from the rest of my life as possible."

"Fine, when you have a moment, we need to speak." I didn't respond to his request because as I walked deeper into the house, I heard the music. Tinkling keys, the tone was sad and I knew it was either her thinking I wasn't coming home, or her instructor was readying her for the concert next month.

Quietly, I made my way to the music room. We loved this space. The room was circular, windows surrounded the walls, and because it wasn't ideal when the sun came in, I had special glass in every window. It dimmed the outside world for me while giving brightness to others.

The doors were opened, and I leaned against the frame. She sat at the piano; I didn't need to see in color to know her dress was white. Her hair, the same gray shade as her father's, fell in gorgeous ringlets down her back. She began gliding her fingers along the piano dramatically as the climax rose. She was outstanding. She made me so proud.

When the last key was struck, she just sat there. Her head lifted and turned, it was beginning to rain and she was drawn to it. She loved sitting in here during thunderstorms. Loved being in the center of the chaos. So much like her father.

Slowly, she walked over to the glass, and I wanted to wrap her in my arms, smell the familiar sunshine and hold tight to my life's purpose. But these moments, when she didn't know I was there, told me the story of how she was feeling. Her hand pressed against the window, followed by her forehead. Sweet girl.

"Your talent puts me to shame," I said, breaking the silence. Her head snapped up and she spun. The layers of white twirled like a flower in the breeze. Whatever sadness she felt washed away when her eyes met mine. Her smile was blinding.

"Papa!" she shouted as she ran to me. My arms were ready for this, and as she made contact, I lifted her higher, relishing the closeness. I breathed her in and prayed that was enough to keep her happy and safe.

"I missed you, sweet girl," I whispered into her hair.

"Are you home for a while now?" she asked, and there was no hiding the tremble in her voice. I was gone for too long, too often. I'd tried to explain it to her, but she was almost eleven. There was only so much she could be brave for.

"Ten whole days."

"You'll be here for my birthday, then?" She hopped down, hope glittered in her familiar eyes.

"I wouldn't miss it for anything in the world." I smiled, thrilled when she returned it.

"Wanna see Daddy?" she asked, and I did. We always went together whenever I was home. She knew a different version of her father than I did, and while she loved him, she knew only the man he was now. It felt like he'd been lost for so long.

"Let's go."

She gripped my hand and she practically vibrated. She was never normally this excited to see her father.

"He's going to be so happy to see you," she said, and the familiar devastation hit my heart.

"Sweetie, I don't think he'll understand. Well, maybe he will, the doctor said—"

She stopped walking so suddenly, it jolted me. "What do you mean?" she asked. Her brows furrowed and there was the cute wrinkle in her nose when she was confused.

I was about to explain her father's condition again, when the sound of another door opening caught my attention.

"Oh!" Patricia, the nurse, squeaked. "They didn't tell me you arrived." She was acting strange. I wasn't a fan.

"What's going on, Patricia?" Tony stepped through another door, his head going from her to me.

Her eyes darted around as if trying to figure out what to say. "One moment. The doctor will speak with you."

With that, she went back the way she came, and a small giggle had me looking down. Tony called my name, but I peered down at her.

"They've been acting silly lately," she said.

"Why?"

She shrugged. "Ever since Daddy woke up."

Chapter Three

Phin

I was told two weeks had passed since I'd woken up. Strange because I never knew I slept. Those two weeks were rough and confusing. I didn't know what was real. It felt like I was listening to voices forever, seeing flashes of light. At one point in those two weeks, I was remembering my eleventh birthday. I remembered it so clearly. My father telling me he was taking me to Disney World, and I'd asked if Poe could come. Then a rush, jolt to a different memory. Poe crying, my mother talking to my father about how they'd keep Poe with them until other arrangements could be made. Yes. His parents, they had died, but that was years ago. He'd wept so hard he'd thrown up. I remembered feeling his pain like it was my own. My mother was on the phone, and I'd overheard her telling someone it was horrific. They were visiting family and were carjacked, shot.

I needed Poe. That was my feeling when my memories took me away from the present.

Beeping noises, clouded vision, muffled words. Where was he? I couldn't vocalize that question for days, and when I did, it was explained to me that he'd be here as soon as he was able.

A few days after I woke, one of my daydreams brought me back to when I was fifteen again, and it was like my brain conjured him up… another memory.

"I don't think they'll let me stay after next year, Phin," Poe said.

"Why not? I think they like you. You're so smart and play that music. Damn, you're gold."

He laughed at my words, but I knew he was right. My father wanted Poe gone. He felt he was a bad influence on me. Probably because I loved him. I loved him so hard it made my bones shake.

"I'll be eighteen and they aren't tied to caring for me anymore. It'll be fine." He nodded like he was positive his lie would feel okay one day.

"I'll go with you, then." I would too, I'd go anywhere with Poe.

He squeezed my hand. "You'll be sixteen. If you go with me, they'll have every living person hunt me down for kidnapping and pedophilia."

He was also right about that. My folks didn't like that I told them I was in love with Poe. I wanted to marry him and live with him. I knew Poe loved me, too, and while we only ever kissed, I knew no other kiss would ever be as perfect.

"You'll wait for me, then? Until I'm eighteen?" I asked, suddenly nervous he'd get away and meet someone else.

"Who'd ever be better than you, Phin?" He leaned in and brushed his lips against mine. "You and me against the world, right?"

Right.

"Mr. Hart, can you hear me?"

It took me almost four days to answer that question. It was like I'd forgotten how to talk, but my brain was screaming.

There was the same nurse and the same doctor all the time. The room I was in didn't look like a hospital, but it was familiar, every ounce of my being knew I should know where I was. *What was happening?* Every chance the nurse got, she would tell me what day and time it was. She'd ask me an hour later what I remembered. I knew there was so much missing. So much I was missing.

I was tired all the time, but when I slept, I didn't dream of things out of the ordinary, I remembered.

"I don't understand," Poe yelled. "How do you feel this is a better choice, Phin?"

"He will kill you, Poe. Don't you understand?" I shook my head as fresh tears fell down my cheeks.

"We run, then." Poe gripped my arms and I wanted to strip him bare. Feel him inside me one more time. I wanted to love him forever and have him love me, too.

"I have to, Poe. Please don't be mad. If something happened to you because of me, I'd never forgive myself and I'd follow after you. Wherever that would be. Even in death."

Poe's eyes widened and his own tears fell, then. "So, that's it? You're going to what? Be with this woman your father wants, marry her, have her babies, and just exist?"

"Yes. Because I will know you'll be alive." I'd be a shell of a man, but if I knew Poe was living and happy, it would be worth it.

"I won't, though, Phin. Every time you walk away, I die a little. Now you're leaving forever? I'm supposed to thrive?"

"You're supposed to try."

That was how these long two weeks were. Flashes of memories. Some pleasant, most painful. I asked for Poe a few times, and the doctor just told me to be patient. He promised me when I was ready. I was, though, I was unbelievably ready.

"Doctor, I need you to come out here. Someone... He's here."

He who? My father? Wait, that can't be.

"Who's here?" I asked. Gladly, the stutter was finally gone. I'd been doing speech therapy for a week, and when they'd determined I'd talk and think just fine, it was a relief. I just couldn't remember why I was here. Who was *he*?

"We spoke about this, Phin. Do you remember?" the doctor, who I remembered was Bailey I think, said.

"The girl. I know her that's my daughter. She's three years older than when I saw her last," I answered, and the doc smiled.

"Yes, what else?"

"She lives here. I see her every day and she plays music for me."

"Wonderful," the doctor said. "Go on."

"I'm twenty-eight. I have a daughter, her name is Adelaide. I'm... I'm married."

The doctor looked over to the nurse and nodded. She walked out, and he was giving me his attention again.

"Who are you married to, Phin? Do you remember?"

The doors opened and it was like everything came rushing back because in the doorway, his hand clutching my beautiful daughter's hand, was my husband. My love, my life, my everything.

"Poe."

"Who is this?" Poe asked, staring at my daughter.

"Her name is Adelaide."

"Okay, why are you here, Phin? I thought you were living your life with your, what is it, wife?"

I shook my head. I'd sent Poe letters for a few years; he didn't write back, I understood why. He was angry, hurt, but he was an artist now. He was amazing and his music was all I listened to.

"You know I never married Pricilla. You know because I wrote you, Poe, every day I wrote you."

He nodded and I was relieved when he held the door open. "Come in, I guess."

I went in and never left.

"Daddy, look who came home. Papa!" Adelaide was jumping up and down, her smile as bright as the sun. "It's gonna be the best birthday ever!"

"Holy shit," Poe said, louder than I think he intended. I wanted to laugh, so much. I did, but I couldn't look away. It was like every emotion was doing a slide show over his face.

Adelaide slipped from Poe's grasp and ran over to my bed. "Daddy, it's gonna be okay now. Papa's here. He makes things better."

He always did before, but by the look on his face, he'd been through so much. More than when I left him before.

"Say something other than that," I said to Poe.

He didn't. He turned on his heel and strode right out of the room.

Chapter Four

Poe

Tony was right there when I stepped into the hallway.

"How long has he been awake, and why didn't anyone contact me?" I spoke in hushed tones because I knew voices traveled, and I didn't want to upset anyone, but I was livid. I wasn't sure if my body or my mind was in shock and just clinging to anything viable. I stuck to my normal setting of *figure out what the fuck went wrong*. I gave strict instructions that any change, no matter how slight, was to be reported to me, and I was going to find out where the fuck up was.

"Poe, you're upset and you have every right to be, but if you'll allow me to explain?" He quirked a brow, not in irritation but in question.

"Very well."

"He woke two weeks ago, but he was very disoriented. He wasn't talking, couldn't. A few times they had to carefully sedate him. I explained to Doctor Bailey that he had to inform you of the change. He feared you'd arrive here and set things back with Mr. Hart. I hated it, I did, but I had another issue."

Tony was calm while he explained, and while I was vibrating inside with anger, excitement, so many feelings, I stood there and listened.

"What other issue?"

"You. You had Adelaide in the center of a human trafficking ring a few months back. No one was getting to her, but the situation was volatile. Fortunately, since that time, no one has followed you home, but you've had so many other fires to put out in Haven Hart since then, I feared they were still watching."

His logic was like ice water being poured over me. I knew that, except—"I still could've been called. Updated."

Tony took a deep breath. "And you would've stayed where you were? Your husband has been in a coma for three years and you'd just be like, 'It's fine, no big. I'll stay here'? I don't think so."

"Tony. I was gone a while this time. Longer than I ever have been. The human trafficking ring situation pretty much finished up months ago. The fires I was putting out had no markings of being connected to it. Contacting me regardless of anything should have been a priority. Why didn't you?"

Tony was an amazing guy, and when I'd hired him I'd specifically told him that while he worked for me, he had to care for Adelaide and Phin above all else. They were his top priority. So when he answered me, I wasn't surprised.

"It wasn't in their best interest. I knew Addy missed you, but Phin had time with her, calmer time. The doc was able to slowly ease him back. They were able to assess his situation."

Of course. "Is he okay? What is he suffering with having been asleep for three years?" Through the years he was asleep, Doctor Bailey, Patricia, and I did our best to keep Phin as healthy as possible. We did exercises to prevent pressure ulcers, atrophy, and infection. We did everything we could think of. In the end, we only had hope.

"He stuttered, was so confused. It took days for him to speak. Physically, he's weak, he'll need a lot of physical therapy to build himself back up, but he's had excellent care and that has a lot to do with why he's doing so well."

Made sense. I'd read up a lot about this, especially to learn what I could do for him. But the longer Phin was in a coma, the chances of him waking up got slimmer. A year ago, I resigned myself to the fact he may never wake.

"I've been going with Adelaide to talk with Phin while you've been away. She couldn't wait to see him. She may have been only seven when he went into the coma, but he's still her father and she wanted to talk to him," Tony said, and all I could do was nod.

"I get it. I just don't like it."

"He's been asking for you." Tony's voice was a whisper.

I turned toward the room where my husband rested. I could hear Adelaide chuckling, and the timber of his voice. It had been so long.

"Very well. Thank you, Tony."

"This place is so far away," I said, looking around the huge house hours away from Phin's family.

"We can't be near them, Poe, you know that. I need Adelaide away from them. If they get their claws in her, I'll be trying to pry her loose forever." Phin had Adelaide on his hip. She was three and the hate of the world hadn't had its chance to touch her yet.

"They'll find out about her, Phin. If anything happens to you…"

He placed Adelaide down on the shiny wood floor. She began wobbling away, but the door was closed in this room so we let her go.

"I know. We need to have safeguards, Poe. We need to be a hundred steps ahead of my family."

I agreed with that. "You have a plan?"

He nodded, his smile half excited, half nervous.

"I ran away from you to save you. I thought being with Pricilla would make my father happy, my family happy. That I, the heir of the Hart fortune, was settling down. But that didn't work. When Pricilla and I moved to Paris, she told me she wanted no part of it. My father and uncle were too terrifying. She was scared, Poe."

I clutched his hands, the tremble sent ripples through my own fingers.

"Then she found out she was pregnant." I knew Phin loved Adelaide, but his expression was devastation.

"I had to smuggle her back into the States, Poe. She didn't want to have the baby there, but she didn't want my parents to know. We ended up in that shitty house I told you about in Alabama…"

I knew this story and I had to interrupt. "Phin, you've told me all this, what are you getting at?"

"Pricilla was so afraid of my family, even after Adelaide was born, she fled, she let drugs and alcohol consume her. Feared they'd force a life on her she just couldn't do. She chose death over my family. And I understand that."

My eyes lingered over the house once more. "What do you want from me, Phin?"

"I need you, Poe. I've always needed you, I love you. Help me protect my daughter and maybe, while you're at it, marry me?"

I stepped into the room, Phin was in the same bed he'd been in for years. Adelaide was on a puffy chair beside him talking a mile a minute about her concert the following month. I only watched for the briefest of moments before Phin's eyes locked with mine. I wasn't one to cry, but I wanted to in that moment. I spent years watching Phin grow into a gorgeous man. I couldn't see the color of his skin, but I saw his muscles grow and the stubble form. He was slightly shorter than me and I loved towering over him. His familiar gray eyes were staring at me, the glimmer I loved attached to a body that I would love watching grow strong again.

"My apologies, Poe, please understand…" the doctor began, but I held up a hand in silence.

"I understand," I said. "Can Phin and I have a moment alone?"

Adelaide giggled and hopped off the chair. She gave him a kiss on the cheek and walked over to me. "He is so excited to see you, Papa," she whispered before she walked out with Patricia and Doctor Bailey.

And then we were alone. The two of us and the muted beeping sound of his heart. My heart.

"Your hair grew," Phin said and all my efforts not to cry failed. I wept, sobbed. And I didn't know how I did it, but suddenly, I was at his bed pressing my face against his chest and his arms wrapped around me loosely.

CHAPTER FIVE

Phin

His hair still felt like silk and it shined like the sea at night. He cried so hard and I felt the years of pain my sleep had caused. Before I slipped into a coma, before the horrible accident, our lives were upside down. Things had come to a head just like Poe had predicted. My coma came at the worst time because he had been carrying everything on his own.

"Oh, Poe, I'm so sorry," I whispered as my fingers slid through his silky hair.

He sniffled against my pajamas and his hand slid under his curtain of hair, likely to wipe his nose. I watched him intently as he lifted himself up. It felt like I hadn't seen him in forever, and while I hadn't, it was hard to explain what my mind went through.

He reached over and grabbed a tissue. He composed himself as best he could before he spoke. "None of this was your fault, Phin."

"All of it was my fault, you know that."

Shaking his head, he sat in the chair Adelaide had vacated. "I agreed to this, Phin, you know that."

I began to talk, only to have a coughing fit. As fast as ever, Poe was up getting me a cup of water, and when a straw was pressed to my lips, I sucked. The relief instant.

"We can talk about all of this later. You woke up after being asleep a long time. I won't be the reason you have some sort of panic attack and something happens to you."

The smile felt amazing. Poe was always the person that in the face of adversity would either walk away when directed at him, step forward for others, or find a way to work through it to better a situation. It's why I left him everything. He'd keep Haven Hart standing, Adelaide safe, and no one would touch him.

"I'm fine, Poe, or at least I will be. I... I have these moments where I feel like you've told me things. But I was asleep."

His eyes widened and he placed the cup down. "You remembered things while you were in a coma? That has to be awful."

"Sometimes it felt like no one could hear me. But it also made me not so lonely. But I couldn't rationalize what was real and what wasn't." I didn't know what he understood about comas, but it was clear no one could truly understand unless they had been in one.

Hollywood does a great job of telling us it's like a blink. One minute here, the next time there, but that's not it at all. It's voices, and smells, it's frustration, and wanting. Sometimes it felt like I was tied down and couldn't get up. I didn't want to tell Poe that, he was already crestfallen over knowing I could hear him all this time.

"The doctor said that while your brain activity showed signs of possibly understanding, there was just no way of truly knowing what you were absorbing." His hand was so close to mine, and I wanted desperately for him to touch me. "Comas are a great mystery to doctors we found out."

"You look so tired, Poe." He did. Gorgeous as ever, but he wore the years on him like they were church confessions.

He chuckled, but it wasn't like fresh air, it was staler. "It's been a long few years."

"What have I missed? What's been happening? Before the accident everything was a sudden nightmare and—"

Poe finally took my hand in his, and that was when I felt the fresh air, the lifeline. "Shh, please don't get worked up or Doctor Bailey will yell at me." The quirk of his lip was sexy, but I knew I worried him.

"I need to know everything, though. Is she okay? Are you? What's going on with my family, with Haven Hart?"

When he pressed his fingers to my lips, I shut up. "I'll tell you everything, but I'll do it my way, and in a way that won't have you suffering a stroke or anything. Do you understand?"

I loved his dark eyes. I didn't always get to see them because he wore his glasses but here, in our home, it was safe. Everyone understood about his eyes, so he'd never worry about it here.

"Fine. But please tell me something now."

He pursed his lips; his eyes narrowed as he thought. "Before your accident, as you know, we had things fairly secure. Things were calm for a while. I was doing meditation with Snow and Teddy." He smiled at the memory. "I don't get to anymore but it's okay, they became good friends."

"I'm glad you listened to me and made some. You needed a life outside of me and Adelaide."

He shook his head. "You and Adelaide are my life, and these last three years you've been nothing but."

Before my accident, I remembered Poe had met Snow and Teddy. I wanted his face to become more familiar in Haven Hart so if something happened, if he went missing, people would notice. He was already painting and some knew of him, but when he told me who he'd befriended, I knew people like Snow and Christopher Manos would keep him safe. The Manos family, while a family linked to crime, brought an odd balance to Haven Hart. I watched them through the years. I knew my father had a great dislike for them but understood that it was better the devil you knew.

Everything went to shit a year later. I knew Poe was talking with others. Involving himself with what my family would call unscrupulous people. But he had it under control, he said. He promised to protect Haven Hart, Adelaide, even me. I trusted Poe with my world. Then it came crashing down.

"There's so much to tell you, Phin, but it's most important no one know you're awake."

That had me incredibly confused. Did my family think I was dead?

"Why?"

He closed his eyes briefly, and when he opened them, I knew I was going to have my world turned upside down.

"To your family, Edward Phineas Hart is in a vegetative state, never to rejoin society. For all intents and purposes, you're dead."

I never used the name Edward. It was a family name, and while on paper I was Edward, to those who knew me I was Phineas, or Phin. It served me well while hiding.

"It was my family, wasn't it? Who tried to kill me?" I'd wondered, as I'd tried to hit the brakes on my car on that perfect autumn day and they'd failed, when my car slid over wet leaves into the embankment; *did my family do this?*

"They found out about a child, Phin. They did exactly what we said they would, they thought by removing you from the equation they could take her and mold her into what the Hart name was meant to be."

That's right. I was on my way home to talk to Poe after I had an argument with my uncle. I had to tell him to keep her at this house. Safe. Then it all went to shit.

"Then what happened?" I asked with bated breath.

"What happened was they quickly found out that by trying to kill you, they made their lives worse. For the last three plus years, I've kept them at arm's length, powerless. Yes, what we did to secure the Hart name, Haven Hart, all the people there, and our little family, worked. But with great cost."

I knew it would, I worried about that. And all these years the burden fell on Poe's shoulders.

"So we're safe as long as they think I'm brain dead?"

He shook his head, and he may as well have been shaking the

world. "No, they're figuring a lot out. There's been whispers, poking, I've had my ear to the ground, and they aren't going to sit idly by and let me hold the keys to the city much longer."

Tendrils of fear crept up my spine. "What do we do?"

His eyes glittered with everything: fear, mischief, joy, sadness, knowledge. "I spent years cultivating a town where things were fair. Not always safe, but when the fires rose, I was able to help wash them away. Your family is going to strike, I know it. It will be soon. But I have a plan. I have people. I just have to hope your family holds off until you're more stable."

"I'm fine."

"Sorry, Phin, but you need to trust me on this. We have to do this right or not only will we perish in the flames, all of Haven Hart will, too."

I did trust him. So I nodded, and the rush of exhaustion hit me, and he sat there until my lids closed and I had a dreamless sleep.

Chapter Six

Poe

As soon as I knew Phin was in a deep sleep, I stepped out of the room in search of Tony. I saw Adelaide and Patricia in the kitchen as I passed. Sara, the housekeeper and cook, was with them and they were baking cookies. I left them to it and went to the security room where I knew Tony would be.

"We need to speak privately, Tony," I said as I entered. I trusted the other guys, but I knew by explaining things to Tony, he could delegate tasks better.

He followed me to my office, and when the door closed, I took a much needed breath. Mere hours ago I was heading home excited to have a birthday party for Adelaide, now everything was chaos.

"Poe?" Tony's voice cut through my internal monologue where I was having a nervous breakdown.

"Right, okay. This whole thing—" I waved my hand in the direction of where Phin slept "—this is a potential war." My heart was racing. I was never expecting to hear Phin's voice again, feel his fingers in my hair or on my skin. I wanted this more than anything, but I had convinced myself that if he slept he couldn't be hurt.

"I agree." Tony took out a tablet. "I've begun increasing security protocols. We may need more bodies, especially on you when you go into Haven Hart. Adelaide is homeschooled, so she's safe here. Her concert next month could be tricky, but hopefully, the Hart family isn't aware of who she is by name. Last intel tells us all the Hart family knows is Phin had a child. You have the only access to the vaults, and every person who works in them was vetted by you and me together. The Hart family doesn't even know who works there."

He was trying to reassure me, but he knew the glass was cracking. When Bryce was discovered to be a mole for Gregor Mims and the human trafficking ring, we speculated he told others or that there were other moles. There was a lot of rumbling lately, and I suspected the Harts knew more than we thought.

"Tony." I held up a hand. "Do you remember when we found out Phin was in a coma?" He nodded. "We went on high alert. We let them think he'd never wake up because it kept them from trying to find and hurt him."

"But they thought the reins would be handed back to them."

"Right," I said. "And that's what gave us the great opportunity to cover our tracks on Adelaide and be sure they never knew of this place."

"But they did find out about her."

I shook my head. "About a child, yes. But the specifics of Adelaide were kept quiet. Not even within the vaults will they find her information. I saw to that."

"But they knew about a child."

That was the issue. "Which means they likely know more about her than we thought." I was pacing the room at this point, thinking out loud. "They tried to get everything: her, the vaults, the money, all of it. But they didn't count on me. They didn't know that not only did I marry Phin, but I had adopted Adelaide. She was mine in every sense of the word."

"And the target on your back grew, Poe."

"Yes. I knew it would. It's why when they approached me, I was ready for them."

And I was so ready for them. In that moment, I was untouchable, but I feared that time was coming to an end.

"I've been watching them, Poe. If they were getting ready to make a move, I'd know. Yes, there's chatter, but nothing about a strike or anything huge." Tony turned his tablet toward me. The Hart family had schedules, and I had access to them all. Nothing new this next month or odd cancellations. As I stared at the calendar, I realized Phin's uncle was on there the most. The rest hadn't been as active, mostly overseas events. I made a mental note to deal with the why of that later.

"But what if they find out that Phin's awake?"

Tony huffed. "How?"

"I don't know. How'd Bryce get passed anyone? It just happens."

He had nothing to say to that. I knew he was beating himself up over it, and it was a low blow on my part.

"I'm sorry, Tony, that was wrong of me. I know you feel horrible."

He slipped the tablet inside his jacket. "I do feel horrible. But more than that, I feel responsible. Had it not been for Black and his people, I don't even want to think what would've happened."

Ahh, yes. Black. I figured I'd ask Tony his thoughts on what Quill had asked for.

"What do you think about Black, Snow, Quill, and Christopher?"

"Besides the fact that three of them have odd names?" He chuckled, and I couldn't help but smile.

"My birth name is Raven, and you all call me Poe. I'm not one to talk."

He shrugged. "Yeah, I guess. Are you asking if they should be brought in on this? Because I told you, they likely should help. You gave that Lee guy the flash drive with maps and info. I'm sure he's going to decrypt it all and realize you're asking for help in your weird way."

"Weird way? Thanks." I heard Adelaide laughing from the

kitchen, and the worry I felt deep in my heart began to thud. "I have to do something. If I wait for the Harts to do something, it won't be a tap on the shoulder, it'll be devastation. I have to get ahead of them."

Tony nodded. "You do."

While I knew I had to talk with Black and Lee and all of them, there was one person I owed all of this to first.

"Tony, I need you to do something for me."

"Anything."

I sat in the chair by my desk, took another deep breath, took out a piece of paper, and wrote as I spoke. "Don't call, just go. We can't risk ears out there. Bring him here. Just him. I will inform him of everything; he has earned that. With him knowing we can go from there, but he deserves to be told before the others." I glanced at the clock. It was late afternoon. God, this day was going fast and dragging all the same.

I held out the piece of paper. "Give him this note when you arrive. The less vocalized out loud the better."

Tony opened the note as I knew he would and read it quickly. "You think Snow Manos is just going to follow me to an undisclosed location?"

I pointed to the note. "He will when he reads that because he'll know it's from me, and he'll realize it's the answers he's been dying to know."

Tony shook his head. "His husband won't like it."

"One thing I've learned about Snow is he doesn't so much ask his husband to do things or for anything. He will come regardless. He trusts me."

"And you trust him?"

I paused, giving thought to Tony's question. Snow and I hadn't always seen eye to eye, especially in recent months, but did I think I could trust him to be there when I needed him? The answer was simple. "With my family's life."

He gave a curt nod and left. I knew he was going to be updating everyone on the unexpected guest, and the house would be aflutter with activity. I had no idea how Snow would react, but I knew even if he was livid, he'd do everything in his power to help me.

Chapter Seven

Phin

"*Holy shit, that feels good,*" *Poe mumbled into the pillow as my tongue swept over his hole. "I see why you like it so much when I do it."*

I chuckled and tenderly bit his ass cheek. "Just because you like this doesn't mean you'll like it when I stick a finger or my dick up your ass."

Whenever Poe and I had sex, and he was balls deep inside me and we were the closest two humans could be, was the best moments of my life. I told him that and he said he felt the same but was curious about feeling it the other way.

"Maybe, but I'm loving this." He moaned as I speared my tongue and jabbed into him. He was harder than stone and I felt so powerful.

I pulled back and reached for the lube. He watched me from over his shoulder, and I winked as I spread a good amount on my fingers.

"You'll tell me to stop if you hate it, right?" I asked.

"I promise."

But he didn't. I licked and fingered him for what felt like forever, and yet, it was only moments. When he rolled on his back, spread his legs in the sexiest wanton way, I climbed up his body until flesh and flesh collided.

"I love you, Phin," Poe said, and while I knew he did, he never said it with so much emotion. We loved each other before we ever kissed. But it was so real.

"I love you too, Poe." Neither one of us had ever slept with anyone, and secretly we were tested just in case because Poe was

paranoid. We wanted to always be bare with each other. So when I pressed the tip into him and his eyes shuttered closed and his breath hitched, I wanted to live inside this man.

He never stopped me and we made love, fucked, did everything we could think of.

I didn't know if it was because every moment we were together might have been our last or because that night we both knew, without a doubt, that we'd never give our hearts to anyone else.

I was jolted awake by a door slamming. I looked around the room, but only Patricia was in here. She sat by the window reading something but didn't show any signs of hearing the door.

"How are you feeling, Mr. Hart? You were asleep an extremely long time." Patricia peered over the book. "Need something?"

"Is Poe around?" I looked over to the clock beside me; I'd been out for more than half the day. It was close to dinner time.

She placed her book down and came over to me, noted what the machines said and then smiled. "He's actually in a meeting with someone right now, but he told me to tell you he'd be in as soon as it was over."

A meeting? In this house? "Is it with Tony or the staff?" She shook her head and began fixing already pristine sheets. "Then who?"

"I'm sure Poe will explain everything. I don't always understand things, and I'd hate if my answer made you worry unnecessarily." Patricia was someone Poe had hired, obviously after my accident. I'd spoken to her a lot since I woke, and I'd found her to be a wonderful woman.

She had short dirty blonde hair, light brown or possibly hazel eyes, and was on the short side. I pegged her as being in her late sixties. I gathered, because she was here all the time, that she wasn't married or anything, but I hadn't worked up the nerve to invade her privacy.

"Fair enough." I saw only a small glass of water and realized I was actually hungry. "Any chance I can eat something?"

"Absolutely. Sara made a delicious butternut squash soup and fresh bread. I'll go grab you some." She made to leave, but I stopped her to ask if Adelaide would be able to eat with me. It felt so strange asking if I could see my daughter, and I realized so much had changed in three years.

"I will be sure to see where she's at." She then left me alone.

The room had a large screen TV, bookshelves filled with literature, there was a piano, cello, and violin. I knew it was all Adelaide and Poe's, and they had a few instruments scattered around the house. More were in the music room, even a harp, but no one really favored that too much. I think Poe got that because his mother loved to play it for him as a child.

It was a huge room made of oak shelves and walls, cranberry colored carpeting, an antique but simplistic chandelier was in here, and the windows brought a lovely light. I wished I could get up and walk there and look at the grounds. It was autumn, Patricia had told me. I loved the colors of the leaves.

"Here we are." Patricia came in holding a tray, and the smells hit my nose the second she rested it on the rolling table and placed it in front of me. "I did seek out Adelaide, but she was covered in paint from helping the gardener with some stone art. She's in the bath right now."

I nodded in understanding and breathed in the aromas. "Smells delicious." I took the spoon in hand, I was still quite weak, and on occasion I'd drop spoons, forks, even a pencil mid-sentence. Patricia hovered and while annoying, I understood.

"I can do this," I whispered, and Patricia smiled. It took me longer than it should, but I managed to eat half the soup and a few bites of the bread before calling it quits.

With a full belly, I hated how sleepy I became. Patricia put the television on, and I laughed when she stopped it at *The Blair Witch Project*. "I haven't seen this movie in years," I said. The moment of nostalgia made tears rise to the surface.

"I can change it." Patricia made to do so, but I stopped her.

"No, it's okay. I'm... I don't understand it. I get oddly emotional lately."

She nodded and sat beside me. "Mr. Hart..."

"Phin."

She smiled. "Very well. Phin, your body, while it doesn't feel like it, went through serious trauma. Comas are still a mystery to people in the medical field, and every person who's woken up from one has a story. Some say it was torture, others say it was like a dream. I'm sure you have your own way of describing what you've gone through. Point is, you need to let your body feel what it feels and heal how it does." She tenderly squeezed my hand. "You're a miracle, Phin. No one thought you'd wake up and here you are, eating soup and talking to me."

"Thank you, Patricia, for helping me and for your loyalty."

She waved her hand and let out an undignified pfft. "Hush. It's been my pleasure."

"I hate just laying here, though. Is there any way I can get in a wheelchair or something and go around the house?"

She was about to answer when the doors opened and Poe stood there. He was stunning and yet, exhausted. Beside him stood another man. One I knew from watching him for a while before the accident. His hair truly was the whitest I'd ever seen, and even from across the room, his eyes glittered a bright blue. Snow Manos was here, and that meant Poe was about to tell me just how dire our situation was.

Chapter Eight

Poe

When Tony texted me two hours later and explained they were flying in, I laughed. I knew Snow wasn't going to want to drive two hours to me when he could take Christopher's helicopter. Tony explained they would drop about half an hour from the house and drive the rest. I had one of Tony's security meet them at the location he provided and waited.

I checked in on Phin, but he was sleeping like a baby. Adelaide was outside helping the gardener. She loved jumping in leaves and collecting pinecones and such. I remembered when she'd got bitten by some bugs last year, and Patricia went crazy, saying things like she may get impetigo because bug bites carried bacteria and a lot of other things about fungus. But, Adelaide would go right back out the next day.

Angel, one of my security, stepped into my office to let me know Tony was pulling up. "Thank you, just have them come in here. Please." He gave me a nod and went to do my bidding.

I sat at my desk and tried to calm my frantic heart. Everyone in this house understood why it was a fortress. Why it could never be penetrated and had to be a secret. When I'd met Snow, I'd never intended to fall into a friendship that felt more like a brotherhood. I'd tried distancing myself when all the questions began. But one disaster after another forced me to intervene, and when the inquiries became constant and everyone became more indignant about my life, and my secrets, I knew something was going to have to be done.

Snow had the ability, I hoped, to be a force that could secure this life I'd built. He had his own heartbreaking backstory, and there was no question he'd understand.

After the brutal death of Snow's mother, his father, who was chief of police where he grew up, sold him to a crime family because he had an eidetic and photographic memory. It came in handy for them, and when they killed his boyfriend and held him against his will at his father's command, Snow was trapped. Stuck in that hell for years, he did everything he could to figure out a way to get out. In the end, he waited for the perfect opportunity to flee. He ran away and landed himself in Haven Hart. For years he lived on the streets, and one night he saved a little boy from a horrible fate. That boy was Simon Manos, Christopher's nephew. Only someone like Snow could thaw the heart of the kingpin of Haven Hart.

Snow and Christopher's story wasn't an easy one, but it was a happy, nonetheless. Every stressful or chaotic situation they got into, they always came out of it together. I helped on occasion, and now I needed my friend's help.

A light tap caught my attention, and I looked up to see Tony and Snow standing there. Snow, ever his curious self, was looking up, down, and around, absorbing it all, never to forget.

"Thank you, Tony, I'd like to speak with Snow alone, and then perhaps, if he has further questions pertaining to security and what you know, the two of you can talk later."

"Okay, holler if you need me." He smiled at Snow who nodded, and then left the room.

It wasn't so much an uncomfortable silence as it was worrisome. Snow wasn't a quiet person. He spoke up for everything he believed in, and on many occasions, gave me a good tongue lashing. To see him walking through my office and not making eye contact with me was jarring.

"Snow?" He jumped when I spoke but turned my way. "Would you like a drink?"

He chuckled, but it held very little humor. "What's the strongest thing you've got?"

Ahh, so he was having trouble with all this. Understandable. I walked over to the small cart with some beverages and poured us each a Jack and ginger ale. I knew he didn't like drinking because of his father, but he wasn't kidding that he wanted a drink.

"Thanks," he said as he took the drink and sipped it. "So, this is really weird."

I couldn't argue with that. "Did you read my note?"

He rolled his eyes at my obviously stupid question. "I wouldn't be here if I hadn't. You have Jason Momoa over there come to my house, tell me he can't say much but to read this thing and to follow him. You're lucky Christopher wasn't home, or Bill for that matter, or I wouldn't have been able to sweet talk Donny into trusting my life choices and going with Aquaman."

I couldn't help but enjoy Snow. He made me smile, and even in the face of deceit, madness, and unbalance, he was loyal. Our relationship wasn't always smooth, and for a short while, we didn't speak. After the death of my assistant, Snow muscled his way back into my life and while shaky, our relationship survived, and we were on better terms. I knew I would be telling him everything today.

"Thank you for coming. I know it's getting late and you'd like to be home, so I won't keep you too long."

He shrugged. "It's fine, I was having a quiet day anyway, and nothing planned this evening. So tell me why I'm here, and where I am, and what the ever loving fuck is going on?"

"Please have a seat, and I'll do my very best to explain everything."

Like his ass was on fire, Snow went and sat. Eager, no doubt, to find out everything I'd coveted all these years.

"Before I begin, you must understand a few things." He nodded as he clutched his beverage to his chest, eyes wide like a child listening to a fantastical tale. "One, you can't tell a soul unless I clear it. Two, these secrets were kept not to be malicious, but to keep others safe. And three, you're here because I need your help."

He took the final sip of his drink, placed it down on my desk and spoke. "There's nothing in this world I wouldn't do for Christopher or Simon, Poe. Even harbor great secrets and unapologetically sacrifice others for their well-being." He sat forward, eyes intently staring at me. "You know this because I asked you to uncover the very thing you're talking to me about today for the men I love."

This was where Snow and I were the same and why he'd understand what I told him today.

"Tony, also known to you as Aquaman…" He chuckled but let me go on. "He has felt I should have brought you and others in a while ago. I wasn't so sure, but now I see that I can't sit on this any longer."

"What others?"

"Aside from you, Black, his men. Basically, I will need your side and Black's side in order to, for lack of a better word, protect this."

Snow was sitting back once more; I knew his mind was doing that rewind thing, playing back everything he knew and trying to piece it all together.

"Just tell me what you have to and I promise you, Poe, I will do everything I can to help you." I knew he would, too.

"We're not so different you and I, Snow. We both love people we'd die for. We're also the same because we both have husbands who are under spotlights, and a child that would be used as bait in a heartbeat."

I let my words sink in for a moment. Snow's eyes widened, his mouth opened and closed like a fish out of water. But he composed himself enough to say, "Yeah, start from the beginning, please."

I sat there for the next while telling Snow the story of how I'd lived on the Hart estate since I was ten. I met Phin when he was a little younger and how he was the best friend I'd ever had. I shared with him about how my family and I immigrated here from Russia, and how the death of my parents had forced the Hart family to take me in out of obligation.

I started to tell him about how Phin's father had approached me just two weeks shy of my eighteenth birthday and told me I had to leave shortly after, but Snow stopped me.

"Hold up." He shook his head, anger obvious in his features. "He practically raises you, but because his son tells him he has tingles over you, you're suddenly dispensable?"

I chuckled, because while I was telling Snow this story, he couldn't truly understand the evil nature of the Hart family to see why this was indeed possible.

"I was always dispensable to them, Snow. Don't you see?" I opened the top drawer of my desk and took out a few keys. I placed them on the blotter, and then pushed them toward Snow.

"What are those?" Snow asked as he pushed the chair closer to the jeweled keys. They were strictly ornamental, but to the Hart family, having them meant power.

"These are the objects that made the Hart family realize that by throwing me away, they gave me everything."

Snow reached out and gently touched the keys, his fingers grazed the gems that were embossed in the gold. He looked up at me, his eyes glittered and there was clarity there. "These are the keys to the vaults, you married the heir to the Hart dynasty, and you have a child with him?" I nodded. "All this time." His voice was a whisper. "Yeah, Poe, I'm going to need to know a lot more."

I understood, but there was something I needed to do first. "I want to introduce you to someone. Then I'll tell you the rest."

When we entered the room where Phin was recovering, I was glad to see he was finally awake. His gaze went from me to Snow. His confusion morphed to realization. But he smiled nonetheless.

Chapter Nine

Phin

"You're Snow Manos," I said when it was obvious the man wasn't going to speak first.

"Yeah... uhh... and you're the elusive Mr. Hart." He inched closer and indiscreetly took in his surroundings: the bed, machines, the opulence of the room.

"Poe hasn't told you everything, has he?" Knowing Poe, he told him just enough and felt it was time to show him me before continuing.

"When does he ever?" Snow mumbled the words, but I heard them easily enough.

"He's had a heavy burden to carry all these years. It's not his fault." I couldn't jump out of bed and block a bullet for Poe yet, but I'd defend him as best I could.

"Don't get so defensive, I understand why." Snow narrowed his eyes as he read the machines, grabbed the folder and read over the medical jargon. I looked at Poe who had a smirk on his face. Clearly this was what Snow did, helped himself to information.

"You're showing great signs of recovery. Hand and eye coordination are getting better every day. Your speech has improved. Physical therapy begins in a few days. That'll be awful for you but necessary." He went on and on, and I felt ridiculous joy at the normalcy of this. Snow could've hit me with a million questions, but instead, he was reading my chart.

"According to this, you were in a car accident a little over three years ago. Broken leg, clavicle, head trauma, blah, blah, blah, that explains the coma, okay... yeah, so wow. Look at you being a medical mystery." He closed the folder and met my eyes. "You are a wanted man, Mr. Hart, did you know that?"

He didn't say it threateningly, just in a way that told me he was aware of my importance.

"And you're here to help me, Poe, and Adelaide, from succumbing to the bad side of that statement."

"Adelaide." He said her name like another puzzle piece was put down in front of him, but the name didn't seem to spark surprise.

"Snow," Poe said, coming up beside him. "I don't want to have to tell this story a million times to those who need to know. I'm telling you because I trust you, and I know you won't forget a word of it. You'll be able to answer certain questions so I don't have to keep repeating myself."

Snow chuckled. "But it's okay if I have to repeat them?"

"Yes, sort of. I have to deal with so much." Poe released a breath. "Snow." He reached over and took my hand. The feeling of perfect connection was like being plugged into life. "This is my husband, Edward Phineas Hart."

Snow turned to me. "Edward."

"It's a family name. I never went by it."

Snow nodded with a smile, then looked over to Poe. "When Atticus asked for the Hart heir's name, you said Phin. You said no one would ever find anything on Phin Hart because he didn't exist."

Poe returned the smile. "Yes, and I knew you'd remember that. I've removed all information on Phin and Adelaide from everywhere. Most people hear Phin and think of it with an F. It was a safe bet Atticus would, as well. But on the off chance someone went so far back and I'd missed it, they'd only find an Edward P Hart. Not even Phineas. It was a safe bet."

"Why not just give a completely false name, then?"

Poe released a breath. "It was a risk, I understand that, but while I felt Atticus wouldn't figure it out, I didn't want to risk Simon or Christopher's life. Phin was in a coma, and if I'd thought Atticus would find him, I wouldn't have been so forthcoming."

Snow shrugged. "No one ever said you were stupid, Poe, that's for sure." My confusion must've shown on my face because Snow explained further. "Atticus Spiros was a piece of shit who kidnapped my husband and Simon. He wanted to have a face to face with you. Poe promised your name, gave him Phin, and then before it all came to blows with the discovery, Atticus was dead and you were safe." I was still confused, but I also knew after being out for three years there was no way I was going to know everything at once.

"I'm sure I have a lot to catch up on, Snow, but first, call me Phin. I'm sure you have a ton of questions of your own."

He nodded and sat in the chair beside my bed. "I know the name Adelaide."

"You sent Quill to my studio to ask about her," Poe countered as he sat on the bed, his hand still in mine.

"She's your daughter?" Snow's eyes were filled with stories, wisdom, and secrets. They were the only thing about him that seemed aged. He couldn't forget, therefore it was a prison in a sense.

"She is biologically mine, yes. But Poe adopted her, so she's his as well." I had no time to beat around the bush, so answering matter-of-factly was my best option.

"Where's her mother?"

Poe took this one. "Pricilla Anderson is dead. She couldn't deal with the Hart family and abandoned Adelaide and Phin. She later ended up dying of a drug overdose."

"And you two married, and then there was an adoption." He wasn't asking anything yet, just catching up. "How did you keep a marriage and adoption from your family?"

"I had the power at the time. My father became ill, therefore everything was handed to me. I was in Paris when the family decided it. Thinking I was with Pricilla and everything was as it should be, they had no reason to think anything was off." Poe squeezed my hand as I spoke. "When I came back, secretly, and Pricilla gave birth, I hid in Alabama. I wasn't sure what I was going to do. My entire family thought I was still in Paris. We stayed there for over a year."

"Then he showed up on my doorstep holding Adelaide. I hadn't seen him in forever, but he was sending me letters. I could never write him back since there was never a return address. But I knew what was happening. Didn't stop me from being an asshole, though." Poe smirked.

"And then you married in secret and adopted in secret… all while in Haven Hart?" Snow sounded like he was mystified.

"When you have all the power, you learn how to wield it," Poe said. "Everyone who works here in this house knows the cost. A few left the Hart estate to be here. We have an attorney who works solely for us, and when we needed things solid, he made them that way. No documents of adoption were in the vaults or in any court."

"So then how…" Snow didn't know what to ask.

"My family did find out about a child. Never who the child was or anything, but they did know one existed, and they wanted her. I was slipping out of their grasp, any chance of getting me back to their way of thinking was dwindling, and they knew I was speaking with Poe again. They thought if they could get her it would be everything. They could take over while she grew up and, in that time, they could mold her to their wills."

"Your accident wasn't an accident, was it?" Snow asked.

"No." It was all I could say. Poe was here when I wasn't awake.

"The Hart family kept hitting walls left and right, and when the things they wanted for Haven Hart went against Phin and my beliefs and would kill this town, Phin kept shooting them down. He had them under a financial allowance, one I fully supported to this day. They were cornered."

"Jesus," Snow whispered, but Poe continued.

"Our attorney told me they were hiring the best of the best to find a loophole to change the way this power worked. But then he told me that as long as Phin lived, there'd be no way."

"But you two were married," Snow said.

"They didn't know that," I answered. "So, the day of my accident my uncle Trenton approached me. He said I had to wake up and stop the games. Told me he'd take everything from me if he had to, in order to obtain control. I knew he wanted money, and it was the first time I wasn't sure what lengths my uncle would go to. I had to get back to Poe and Adelaide. I needed to let Poe know that my uncle was gathering information, and that we had to secure all we had. I knew my family had taken down corporations before, turned millionaires into bums. I had to make sure that didn't happen to us." I was sure Poe had figured all that out by now. He didn't show signs of shock, just sadness. "I knew my uncle was going to do everything to freeze assets, do whatever he had to, and threatening Poe and Adelaide's future was my weakness. But violence?" I shook my head. "It's so hard for me to accept my uncle would do that."

"And on your way here to tell Poe the new information you gathered, you crashed." Snow was piecing it together.

"And when he was in a bad state, they tried to swoop in," Poe responded. "But by then, I had the power being his husband and they didn't realize that."

"Now, I'm not saying this should happen, but why not just kill you and Adelaide and take it all, or even just you and take the girl?" Snow asked a valid question.

"I figured out quickly what the plan was and why Phin was in a coma. I discovered they did this. So I built safeguards. I changed the way the dynasty ran. I told them at any sign of betrayal or anything else, I'd open the vaults to the public and their secrets would be exposed. But just in case that failed, in the event of my death, power wouldn't go to any Hart family member. So, if they kill me, the Hart name dies."

This was something I didn't know.

"If you die, where does it go?" Snow asked.

"In the event that I die, the dynasty is split. The vault keys will go to you, Snow. The finances will be handed over to Black. The technology and geographical info will go to Lee."

I was shocked he'd done all of this on his own, but it made perfect sense. While they were criminals in the simplest of terms, they valued this city. They wanted it to stand.

"Us?" Snow stated in wonderment. "They knew this? You had our lives at risk?"

Poe shook his head. "No, calm down. They didn't know *who*, that was what terrified them. They had no idea, just that someone else would have the power. It was a better the devil they knew sort of thing. Not knowing where your secrets would land is scarier than knowing who has them."

"So, you were awake and everything when I met Poe?" He was talking to me now.

"Yes, with my family figuring out I was talking with Poe again, I needed him visible. He truly is your friend. He went out to meet people and met you, that was coincidence but also perfect. I hoped they wouldn't hurt him if he had people who would miss him."

Snow nodded. "And around the time of the accident was when you began slipping away from us," he said to Poe.

"It was a lot, Snow. And I was…"

"Alone," Snow finished. "There are still unanswered questions. But I get it. It's a lot to take in, but I understand why you've done it all. Now I need to understand something else, if you have this power and protection, why do you need me at all?"

"My family is becoming desperate is my bet. And when that happens, it's bad."

"I've heard some rumblings. And after Bryce, well, I'm not so sure there are as many secrets hidden as I thought."

I had some catching up to do on Bryce and what that meant, but I'd ask Poe when we were alone.

"And by willing mobsters and assassins the city, in the event of your death, you've made the place we all live a battleground." Snow stood and began to pace.

"No, Snow." Poe stepped in front of him. "I was trying to avoid a war."

Snow chuckled darkly. "Oh, dear Poe, no matter how this goes, a war is exactly what you've started."

Chapter Ten

Poe

I offered for Snow to stay the night, but he said he wanted to get home and discuss this with Christopher. He promised to contact me the next day with a semblance of a plan.

"Poe?" Phin's voice called to me down the hall. Snow had just left with Tony to go to the helicopter. I entered the room and he was sitting up, a small smile on his beautiful face.

"I know I have a million things to catch you up on. You learned a lot there with Snow and—"

He cut me off with a laugh. "Please, I didn't expect you to sit on your hands while I slept here. You did everything you had to, to keep Adelaide, me, and Haven Hart safe. I don't fault you, nor do I question you."

I sat on the bed beside him, fingers linked. "I missed you so much, Phin." His eyes were sorrowful and I ached to make the sadness disappear, but he had to understand how his absence nearly broke me.

"Tell me," he whispered, and it was like the key was turned and the door opened.

"All our lives it was always we. You and me against the world. When your dad yelled at you, we would go to the weeping willow and throw rocks in the water. You yelled and pretended the liquid was his face."

"And you did the same."

I nodded. "When things became dangerous and we parted, it nearly destroyed me. I clung to the letters you sent to me. Each one was a bandage I prayed would stop the painful hemorrhaging of my heart."

A tear slid down his cheek, and I hated how my words hurt him, but if we were to move past this, he had to know everything.

"With your family, everything that came with them, we stood united. And then... you were just gone. I was alone and..." The lump in my throat made it hard to speak, and I had to take a sip of his water. "They were like a tornado, Phin, and I was in the center. I didn't get out unscathed."

He furrowed his brow as his eyes took in every inch of me he could. Searching for the wounds he'd never see.

"I didn't always know what to do. I would sit beside you as you slept and ask, no beg, you to tell me what to do. I wept and was angry sometimes. I needed you so much and I hated your family, Phin. I'm talking Satan levels of hatred."

He gripped my hand so tightly as my own tears dripped onto them.

"I never wanted them to ever have control again. I wanted them to feel the soul-crushing, all-consuming pain they caused me. When I signed everything over to Snow, Black, and Lee, all the people your family sneered at, I knew even though I may be dead when they found out, it would be a killing blow. And I began to welcome death in that very moment."

"No," Phin sobbed. "Never, Poe. Death is never better than life, us. What about Adelaide? What if you died and I died, what would happen to her?"

This was the part I didn't tell anyone, yet. "That was the hardest choice to make. Where would a girl like Adelaide thrive? Where would she be loved the way she should, and protected the way she needed?" I had to chuckle at the clarity of my choice.

"Who?"

"There are only two people I know who have the ability to be everything she would need. Riordan and Teddy."

Phin's eyes widened. "I know Teddy. Riordan works for Black, right?"

"That's right. You don't know what happened. Teddy and Riordan married and have a little girl named Rosie. Riordan left the assassin business with Black and is working security. But he's just as terrifying as ever. Teddy, he's just pure love, Phin."

He smiled as a few more tears slipped down his cheeks. "They'd love our girl?"

I inched forward until I was a breath away from his face. "Never as much as we do, but yes. She'd be safe and loved with them."

"I trust you."

While they were words I enjoyed hearing from him, I needed to hear three other ones in that moment.

"I love you, Phin."

"And I love you, Poe. Please, please kiss me. I feel like I've been waiting forever."

I tenderly brushed my lips against his, and before I pressed them together, I whispered, "I have been waiting forever."

Some people describe a kiss like it ignites a fire inside them. That it spurs you on for more. Not this. This was a jump start straight to every inch of my body. Like stars aligning and the constant buzzing in your ears finally quieting. It was life, death, love, fear; it was everything.

He tangled his fingers in my hair as I cupped his cheek, still damp from his tears. He opened for me and I slid my tongue into his mouth, and for the first time in over three years, I breathed.

A tiny throat clearing had us reluctantly pulling away. Adelaide stood a few feet from us, a shit eating grin on her face and a twinkle in her pewter colored eyes. My life was always shades of gray, but these two were the best ones in my opinion.

"Hi, sweet girl," I said, and she laughed.

"You're kissing and I didn't want to interrupt. But…" She looked toward the door and we followed her gaze to where Tony stood. "It's later than normal, but Sara said food is ready and

Tony said to tell you Snow is gone now, and I don't know what that means because winter hasn't even started."

Phin chuckled and god, it was the best sound ever. "Snow is our friend and I hope to introduce you to him."

Her eyes widened. "Does he have any kids?"

Of course, she'd ask that. While she was homeschooled, and there were a few kids she knew through music, she never hung out with many. It was always too dangerous.

"He does. He's older than you, though. But I have some more friends with kids. I'd love if you would meet them."

She nodded enthusiastically. "When, oh could they come here on my birthday?"

"Sweetheart," Phin spoke softly. "I've missed you, can we celebrate it just us this year? And maybe, after we all meet and if we like each other, we can have a party once Daddy is up and moving again?"

She looked crestfallen for a moment, but she'd had a different upbringing. We had to explain things to her for her safety. She didn't ask for this life, but she loved living it. She understood.

"Okay, Daddy, that's fair." She walked over and kissed Phin's cheek, and when I leaned down, she kissed mine. "Come on, I'm hungry."

I was about to say this wouldn't work because Phin couldn't get up when Patricia came in with a state-of-the-art wheelchair.

"Poe, why don't you go with Adelaide? I have to do a few things and then, Tony, perhaps you can assist me by lifting Phin into the chair when I'm done?"

Tony nodded and stepped farther into the room. "Of course."

"I'd like to carry him," I said. I'd wanted to hold Phin for so long and—

"Poe," Phin said. "I want to get cleaned up and looking my best for you and Adelaide. Then after dinner, I'd love it if you'd carry me around the house." He gave me a cheeky smile and I rolled my eyes. He wanted dignity. He didn't want me to see him with a catheter or whatever he considered to be ugly about himself.

"Fine." I pressed my lips to his once more, took Adelaide's hand and walked with her to the dining room.

Chapter Eleven

Phin

Christmas music played softly through the speakers in our music room. It was our first Christmas in this house. Adelaide was fast asleep after hours of playing, baking, laughing, and too many cookies. I wanted this moment with my husband. They were few and too far between. If he wasn't extinguishing fires made by my family, I was. Many nights we spent apart. Not today, though.

"Dance with me?" I held my hand out to Poe who was sipping the delicious spiked eggnog that was his mother's recipe. I loved the blissed out, slightly tipsy glimmer in his eyes. He wasn't carefree often enough.

"You want to dance to 'Silent Night'?" He chuckled.

"I want to dance to anything and everything with you, Poe."

His smile faltered briefly, and I knew he understood the need for these seconds. He placed his cup down and his warm hand slipped into mine.

We danced to "Silent Night" and "Oh Holy Night" before either of us spoke.

"I love Christmas," I said.

"What is it about it that you love?"

I rested my head on Poe's shoulder, smiling when his long hair brushed over my cheek indicating he was leaning in.

"The magic and possibilities, I think."

He huffed good naturedly. "You think?"

We stopped dancing and I pulled back to look at him. "The magic that every kid holds on to. Not every kid gets to witness it but many do. And every year more do, will in the future."

He smiled so brightly, all for me. "That's why you wanted to start the Rainbow Hart Charity Ball every Christmas season."

"It's just something I could do." I pressed my hand against his cheek, the feeling of his soft lips on the palm of my hand as he turned to kiss it warmed me. "Thank you for helping me keep it going."

His dark gaze sparkled with love and slight inebriation. "You'd walked the streets of Haven Hart for years before you fled and no one ever knew it was you. I wonder if someday you'll be able to walk among the people you anonymously love and give everything to, and they'll know who you are?"

"I don't do any of this for praise."

He kissed my palm again. "I know. It's one of the many reasons I love you, Phin."

"I often wonder if my grandmother was still alive if things would be different?" Camille Hart was the kindest, loveliest, and most honest woman I'd ever known. She was the moral compass of the Hart family. When she'd passed away, it was like the demons from below surfaced and things became cold.

"Your grandmother made sure you gained control after your father. Ironclad for a reason. She did that because I think she knew the coldness that was there. She couldn't get around your father but she knew you'd make it all right again." Poe pressed his lips to mine and I breathed him in.

"And we need to make sure it always stays the way she wanted," I whispered against him.

"We will."

"There he is," Poe said happily as Patricia rolled me into the dining room. The head of the table was left open for me, and just being out of that room felt like cement blocks were lifted off my chest.

"Hi, Daddy," Adelaide smiled, and I couldn't stop the giddy happiness that bubbled out of me. I was so happy in this moment. I had no idea what tomorrow or a week from now would be, but seeing the loves of my life in an almost normal setting, waiting for me, being alive, I was beyond excited. Of course, my laughter made her laugh, then Poe. Soon laughter filled the room which consisted of Patricia, Tony, and a few others as they all joined in.

We weren't a typical family, we made this what it was. Each one of them had sacrificed for Poe, Adelaide, and me, and for that I'd love them like my blood.

"What's for second dinner?" I asked as Patricia locked the chair and Poe seemed confused. "I had soup a couple of hours ago." He nodded.

"Apple chicken, mashed potatoes, asparagus. I think there's a sauce of some sort," Poe said, jokingly. "I try not to involve myself in the affairs of the chef."

I chuckled and watched as Poe filled my plate. I was glad when no one helped me eat. Aside from Patricia cutting the chicken because I still needed more strength, I did it myself. No one laughed or even regarded my pace.

"We don't normally eat this late," Poe said, and I looked at the clock.

"Oh my god, it's almost ten."

Adelaide laughed. "I took a nap. It was such a long day, Daddy. But Papa wanted to eat with you. So did I."

"The day got away from me. To think, this morning I was painting in my studio, talking with Quill, and then all this." He gestured toward the table, me, the whole room. "I'm sure it'll hit me hard later."

I furrowed my brow and stared at the rest of the food on my plate. "Hit you hard?"

Poe glanced over at Adelaide who was telling Tony a story about why she wanted a horse for her birthday. He told Patricia we'd be right back and wheeled me out of the dining room so we could have a private moment.

He kneeled in front of me and spoke softly so our words wouldn't travel. "Phin, over thirteen hours ago I didn't know I'd be talking to you. You all knew for weeks. In the span of those hours, my heart beat again for the first time in three years, I confessed everything to Snow Manos, and had to figure out the security of the situation. I'm going to crash after this."

I nodded. "I get it." We could hear Adelaide was still talking about horses, and Tony's deep laughter made me smile. I leaned into Poe, glad when he met me halfway. "I really want to sleep in our bed together."

Poe's eyes widened. "I promise you, Phin, as long as I'm in this house and sleeping, you're going to be beside me."

And now I was crying, again. "Thank god, I wasn't…"

"You weren't what?" Poe gripped my hand fiercely.

"I don't know if I'll walk again, I'm a mess, I lost a lot of muscle mass, I'm… I'm not who I was before the accident."

Poe went from concern to rage in an instant. I saw the fire blaze behind his dark eyes. "You're exactly who I fell in love with years ago. I know you'll walk again and if you don't, I'll fucking carry you, Phin. You're gorgeous to me. I could paint a thousand murals and never get close to your beauty. I could play a million songs, and none would sound as amazing as your laugh." He pressed his hand against my chest. "I love this, what beats in here. Love me forever in whatever form, and I promise to love you a million times more than that."

I was desperate for this man in front of me. I wanted to kiss his flesh, ravage his body. I wanted to feel him moving inside of me. I'd fight harder than I'd ever fought for anything to be able to stand beside him again.

"I don't have those fancy words, but know I'd challenge you on the loving more part."

He chuckled and we stayed there a few more moments enjoying each other. When the laughter in the dining room got louder, Poe took me back in and soon we finished up dinner. Patricia and Sara helped Adelaide get ready for bed. I couldn't tuck her in or anything, so Tony helped me get ready for bed with the help of a few others.

When the house was at rest, Poe lifted me out of my chair and placed me on our bed, being careful not to disrupt my stupid catheter.

"Tomorrow I'll carry you around the house, I promise." He kissed me before going around to his side.

"Okay." Sleep was beginning to push its way in, and I let it take me as Poe rested his head against my chest.

Chapter Twelve

Poe

When I woke the following morning, it was with a jolt. My mind went in a hundred different directions. *Was this real? Did Phin really wake up? Does Snow know everything? Did we have Adelaide's birthday?*

My whole life was in a spin, and while it likely only took a minute, it felt like I was being spun in a cyclone forever, until the chaos settled and the reality came smacking me in the face.

"Are you okay?" Phin's sleep addled voice called to me, and when his eyes blinked trying to clear his own cobwebs, I released a breath.

"Yeah. Bad dream," I answered as I settled back against the pillow.

"More like you weren't sure if yesterday was a dream." Phin knew me too well. I couldn't lie to him.

"Something like that." Turning, I came face to face with him. "We got Adelaide a pet for her birthday, by the way. Sara is going to pick it up and bring it here the morning of her birthday." I had to change the subject to something that calmed my frantic heart.

"I see." He smiled. "What sort of pet are we talking about?"

"I went back and forth. She doesn't favor dogs since Corey's lab jumped on her a couple of years ago. She was scared and fell back into a puddle of mud."

Phin chuckled. "So it's not that she's afraid, she just doesn't like them because now she thinks they're all menaces."

I nodded. "So, then, she's been going on about a horse. Corey said he'd happily help since he worked with his dad for years at your family's place. But we don't have a stable, and

I'm not dealing with bringing even more strangers into our lives. If horses are what we want, it'll be a thing outside of a birthday."

Phin had a permanent smile. Normally, I would ask a person why they looked so happy, but I already knew. He was catching up on his daughter and my life and he liked hearing it all. I loved telling him. I felt this need for him to be on par with me, like it would ease the ache of him being gone so long.

"Your argument is sound, Poe, but I still don't know what pet we got her."

"Then, I thought about sugar gliders." He chuckled and shook his head. "Exactly, I know nothing about them and I don't need something new in my life right now. And let's be honest, Addy is going to be asking a million questions about them, and I wouldn't be able to tell her anything."

"I see we're playing 'let me tell you everything I didn't get' first."

Bumping his shoulder, I continued, "Ferrets were a no-go because Sara is afraid. Same with any sort of rodent, and as she's cooking our food, I will not piss her off."

"I agree with Sara. They scare me."

Poe chuckled. "So, very long story short, she's getting a cat."

Phin's head popped up. "All that suspense and she's getting a cat? I was ready to hear you say you got her an anaconda or something."

"Ha ha ha, look who has jokes. No. I don't do reptiles. But this cat is special."

His eyes widened and I knew something sarcastic was about to come out of his mouth. "Does it know the answers of the universe, or maybe it cleans and does homework?"

"I'm going to gag you." I laughed.

"Promises promises." There was a tingling in my belly. I wanted this man so much in every way. I knew we were far from being able to have the raw physical contact we wanted, but people needed goals.

"Anyway, I'm moving on before you make my morning wood any more of a nightmare."

"Put my hand on your cock, Poe."

The sudden deepening and need in the way Phin spoke almost made me choke on air.

"I... what?"

He laughed and I saw the sheet rustle. He was slowly moving his arm. He wasn't very strong, but he had arm and hand movement and that would grow with physical therapy.

"I need to touch you, feel you. Please."

"What about the cat?" I asked dumbly, and he huffed good-naturedly.

"We can talk about it later. Help me."

I wanted to touch, taste, and surround myself in Phin, but I couldn't do any of that until he was cleared and he hadn't been. So, we would do what we could to be infinitely closer.

I pulled the sheets and comforter back, showing him how prominent my erection was in my sleep pants. Phin's breath hitching at the sight was proof in itself how desperate we both were.

"More," he said.

I lifted my ass up and pulled my pants off. Pre-come glistened at the tip and the gentle caress of Phin's fingers on my hip as he tried to reach almost made me explode.

"I can't," he said. He could lift his arm but couldn't keep it raised for an extended period, yet. I grabbed it and wrapped both our hands around my throbbing shaft. In the same moment, we both moaned.

"Fuck," I said and Phin hummed.

Years. It had been years. I never cheated or thought about cheating on Phin. If he had died, I never would have been with another soul. This man was my everything, and the only one who would ever touch or see me this way.

"Move us," he begged.

I started slow, until my pre-come was sliding down creating easier slickness.

"Yeah, baby, faster." Phin's words were killing me.

I moved faster and faster until my back was arching and come was shooting all over my stomach, chest, and our hands.

I didn't release us from my spent cock. We just breathed and I waited until the fireworks behind my eyelids subsided.

"Shit, Poe, we need to talk to the doctor today. I need to know when you can fuck me."

The laugh burst out of me and soon Phin was in hysterics beside me. "That will be my first task of the morning," I said as I reached for the tissues beside the bed.

After we were cleaned, and my sleep pants were back on, I called for Patricia. Together the two of us were able to bathe and dress Phin. I was glad when she informed me of a physical therapist coming to meet with Phin and me. Phin didn't want to wait and Patricia knew this, so she asked the therapist to come as soon as possible and he was amenable. He'd be arriving shortly.

"Were they vetted?" I asked after Phin was securely placed in the wheelchair.

"No, Poe. Tony decided to take a stranger off the street, ask him his favorite color, if he puts toilet paper over or under, and if he was a lefty or righty. Then let him in," Phin answered, much to Patricia's enjoyment.

"Fine. I'm not talking to either of you now," I said as I made my way to the closet to get clothes for myself.

"Sure. We'll see," Phin answered, but I was in the closet pulling clothes down. I chose a black long sleeved thermal shirt, black jeans, and black boots. I liked the color. Black, gray, and white were my life, but I favored the darker shades over the lighter. I had many long black jackets I tended to wear all the time. Some light, some heavy, some designer. Goth chic was what Sara told me once. But when I was home, I opted for casual comfort.

"We'll head to the dining room for breakfast, and see you down there," Patricia said, and I just grunted.

I was just finishing getting dressed when my cell phone vibrated. Snow's name appeared and I answered, nervous what response I'd receive.

"Good morning, Snow."

"It's too early, if I'm being honest, but my husband woke me at six to talk more about what we discussed. So, of course, after that he left and now I'm wide awake." This was typical Snow. No hello just, here's what's on my mind.

"And what did Christopher have to say in regard to your morning conversation?" Glancing out the window, it seemed to be an overcast day. Hated by many, but for me, it was perfect.

"He wants to meet, of course. He wasn't thrilled, if I'm being honest. But I told him more deets that I don't want to say over the phone because ears are everywhere." Snow was a very smart man, and it was one reason he was my most trusted friend.

"Fair enough. Can we meet Monday, here? I can't do anything before, then." I would have explained to Snow it was Adelaide's birthday Sunday, but I didn't want to over the phone.

"I'm sure you have a reason you want to wait a couple of days and can't tell me over the phone, so Monday it is. Also..." There was a pause and I had a feeling he was trying to say something without saying too much. "I need a way for you to tell me all the people you need to come with me."

Ah. "Bring everyone."

"That's vague, and yet precise at the same time. How'd you manage that?" He chuckled.

"I'll get Tony to send you a list. It should arrive sometime today. There'll be a separate note for a certain couple I'll ask you to give them when you speak to them."

"Fair enough. I'll do your bidding, and I suppose I'm going to have to convince all these people?"

"If anyone can do it, you can." That was the truth. Snow could convince a woman in white gloves to buy a ketchup popsicle.

"Okay, fine. Get me the list, and I'll call you as soon as I know how well the convincing went."

"Okay. And thank you, Snow."

"Yeah yeah." He hung up and I smiled. I should've trusted him long ago. But we were where we were now, and I could only hope the others would be on board.

Chapter Thirteen

Phin

Breakfast was pleasant, and it felt more normal than dinner the night before. Adelaide's tutor was arriving an hour later, and then she had music practice. Poe and I were meeting with the physical therapist this morning and I was eager. I wanted to walk, wash my hair; I wanted to wrap my fingers around Poe's cock and pump it without help.

"Phin?" Doctor Bailey called to me from the dining room entrance. "I was hoping to check you over before physical therapy and then after."

Poe pushed me toward the room I called the Coma Room. Since everything was set up there, it was easier to just keep it that way.

"You have assistance now," Doctor Bailey said with a smile as he glanced at Poe. "I'm removing the catheter. Your eating is better. I still demand you watch your substances. Dinner last night went down better than a week before. This is the improvement I like to see."

I wasn't a fan of having a tube in my dick, and it was awkward this morning pumping Poe's cock while mine had a tube in it. Poe didn't say anything; he didn't even look. I had it covered pretty well, but I wanted it gone.

"I'll take all the improvements I can." I was excited to get back to normal.

"You could still have bladder spasms, there are issues we need to watch."

Poe stepped forward. "We'll watch and report everything.

Recovery is only as successful as the confidence the patient has. Making him feel more himself will make him *be* more himself."

The doctor nodded and I was happy when Poe linked our fingers. Removing the catheter wasn't my idea of a fun Friday sort of thing, but when it was out, I felt relieved.

It wasn't long after the doc left, the physical therapist arrived. His name was Elliott and he was adorable. He had dark brown hair, light brown eyes, and an "everything is going to be fine" kind of smile. We found out he was actually Tony's cousin, and that explained why he was there at all.

We didn't do much exercise. We mostly spoke about goals, expectations, and did some stretching. He stated how pleased he was with the care I was given while in the coma. By the time Elliott left, I was exhausted.

"I have some things to do, but how about we go around the house as I promised, and then you sleep while I get stupid shit done?" Poe said, and I hated I couldn't help yet, but was too tired to argue.

"Sure."

He carried me around the first floor and told me, finally, about Adelaide's birthday present.

"She's a Scottish Fold breed of cat. Truly adorable. I did a lot of research, and she'll be good with her. She's a kitten, so I imagine a lot of training will be required, but it won't be a problem. We have enough hands to help her."

"I have no idea what a Scottish Fold looks like, Poe." I chuckled when he seemed stunned, as if that never occurred to him.

"We can stop at the office right around the corner. I'll pull it up on the computer." When we arrived there, he gingerly placed me in his office chair, and I was thrilled when I was able to keep upright. I felt my body and I could move it, but with no strength, I didn't have the ability to support my weight or walk just yet.

"Here, I have pictures of the one she's getting." He leaned over me, his dark hair shone like a midnight sea, his scent was like home, and for a moment I enjoyed the closeness. Until he pulled away, and on the screen was the cutest kitten I'd ever seen.

"Oh," I whispered in awe. She was chocolate brown with golden eyes, her ears were bent forward and down toward the front of her head. She was almost owl-like. There was no question where the Fold part of her breed came in.

"She's precious, isn't she?"

"Addy will love her." I looked up, left breathless by the content happiness on Poe's face. "Thank you."

His dark eyes met mine. "For what?"

"Everything, all of this, Poe. You've kept us alive and safe. And I know I feel like I keep saying it over and over again but…"

"You do, so stop." His tone was like a whip. Not angry, just precise. "I did what I had to do, what you would've done. Let's just move forward."

I said no more. Poe lifted me in his arms and we continued our walk. At the top of the stairs, a wheelchair waited and Poe sat me in it.

Not much had changed from before I slept. Touch-ups, but that was all. Adelaide's room was now lavender and no longer pink, but that was it. By the time we reached the bedroom, I was ready to crash. Poe helped me into bed, and my head barely hit the pillow before I was asleep.

For the rest of Friday and all of Saturday, it was exercises, birthday party prep, and mundane activity. I knew we weren't broaching the subject of my family until Monday, so I promised I'd enjoy this peace while it lasted.

Sunday morning came with a bounce. Adelaide jumped on

Poe and my bed with an, "I'm officially eleven," cheer that had Poe and I laughing.

"I heard Sara was making you birthday pancakes," Poe said, and Adelaide fist pumped the sky. I was so happy, and seeing the two people I loved most in the world being equally as thrilled, it relaxed me. "Head on down and we'll join you in a few."

She gave us each quick kisses and was off.

"I can't wait to run after her," I said as I propped myself up.

"Elliott said you were a fast study. Told me your arm strength was impressive." Poe slipped out of bed, his black silk pajama pants were teasing me horribly. His chest was bare, pale, but beautifully toned. I wanted to lick him, touch him, devour him.

"Soon," Poe said as he came to my side of the bed. "I know that look in your eye. As soon as we get the all clear, we won't get out of bed for a week."

"Promise?"

"Trust me, Phin, I want you as much as you want me."

I wasn't sure how true that was, but I smiled nonetheless. He helped me get ready for the day, and half an hour later, we were stuffing our faces with the most delicious pancakes ever.

"So, Addy," Poe said as he placed his napkin over his plate. "Since it's your birthday, I bet you want a present."

Her silverware clinked as it hit the plate. "Yes, oh yes, yes, yes. Please, can I have it now?"

Everyone in the dining room chuckled, and Poe nodded toward Tony who walked out. Likely to get the kitten.

"Very well." Poe stood and walked over to the door Tony had exited. A moment later, an obvious cat crate was handed to Poe.

"You got me something alive?" Adelaide shouted and ran over to Poe. "I'm so excited right now."

Poe placed the carrier on the table and lifted the door. The tiniest kitten stepped out. She sniffed, searched, and when Adelaide started crying tears of joy, the kitten let out the most adorable, most pathetic little meow which had Addy scooping her up.

"Oh, thank you, Papa and Daddy." She one arm hugged Poe, then came over to me to do the same. The kitten was already swatting at her hair which made her giggle.

"You have to name her," I said as I petted the kitten with my finger.

"Can I take her in my room and play with her for a little while? Maybe a name will come to me?"

There were a few hours before any celebration happened and I nodded. "Go ahead. I can't wait to hear what you name her." She hugged me and Poe once more and walked slowly out of the room.

"I can go with her, in case she has any issues," Sara said. "The litter box is set up, and I should show her that the kitten needs to know that."

"Thank you, Sara," Poe said.

After everyone cleared out, Poe sat beside me. "I doubt we'll see much of our little girl today." He wasn't sad, he had a brilliant smile on his face. "I love seeing her so happy."

"I do, too."

He pressed his lips to mine, and for a few minutes, it was just him and me and this kiss.

Chapter Fourteen

Poe

Sunday was a day of celebration; cake, laughter, and forgetting. For that day, there was no impending war, no chaos. There was a kitten who loved to climb up people's pants, frosted cake with vanilla filling, gifts for a girl who deserved more but wanted for nothing, and Phin. He was there laughing right along with us. Like a dream come to life.

But soon enough the sun rose, and Monday began. Reality was here and Snow was about to call. I received a brief text Sunday telling me he got everyone on the list to agree to come here on Monday. The letter to Teddy and Riordan explaining the importance of their arrival was delivered. Now I awaited a call from Snow.

Nine o'clock struck and my phone vibrated.

"Good morning, Snow."

"Sure it is," he said and I chuckled. "I felt it best we all not descend on your secret sanctuary of solitude all at once. So, I'll arrive with Chris at twelve, then every half-hour someone else will arrive. This will take some time, so I hope you have rooms there."

"Rooms?" What was he talking about?

"The last people are going to arrive around two. You're going to wrap it all up in a few hours and kick everyone out? We can't all fly and drive out of your place in one go, Poe. Holy obvious!"

He made a valid point. "I have a few spare rooms. I can't keep everyone comfortably."

"Meh, I'm not worried. We need to iron things out. I don't know if we'll all ever be in a room together again. It's like putting every government official in one place. It's a recipe for assassination."

"True. Very well. I'll alert my staff. Tony is my head of security, as you know. He'll be the one arranging everyone's arrivals whether they're flying or driving. He'll contact each party."

"That's your rodeo, cowboy. Have fun with it."

"Thank you, Snow. See you soon."

After hanging up, I let Tony know everything that was going on, and he went into serious mode and went to do what had to be done. Sara agreed to occupy Adelaide until it was time for her to meet everyone. That was something I was nervous about. Snow agreed to bring Simon to help put her at ease by having another person closer to her age there. He was thirteen, almost fourteen now, but still better than a bunch of adults.

Phin was quiet as I explained everything, and I knew he too was worried about the outcome. But whatever came our way, we'd deal with it. We always did.

Together we went into Adelaide's room, sat down and let her know about the visitors we were having and how Sara would be with her until it was time for her to come down.

"Will there be any kids?" She was petting her kitten she gleefully named Countess Cocoa Puff.

"My friends Snow and Christopher will be bringing their son Simon. He's thirteen."

She smiled. "That's great. Hope he likes cats."

And that was that. She took things in stride and I was happy for that.

We got word around twelve that Snow and Christopher's helicopter landed at the same place Snow had arrived during his previous visit. A car was sent and Phin and I waited in the grand room. It was big enough for everyone and welcoming.

Sara had a lovely setting of snacks, and there were drinks of all sorts. Phin asked to be placed in a wingback chair by the window. Even if others guessed, he didn't want people to know he wasn't one hundred percent. Either way, he was dressed casual but crisp: black pants, white button down, and a pair of black dress shoes—when I was asked to pick things out, it was all black and white. He was shaved and looked great. Not as built as he used to be, but he'd get there. None of them knew what he'd looked like before all of this, anyway.

The sound of tires on gravel was like a gong being hit. It was going to be a long day, and we were going to have to get through it; hopefully, ending it with everyone on our side. If I had the backing of Christopher Manos and all of Black's people, there was a good chance I'd be able to end the Hart family's insanity.

Christopher Manos was a man who entered the room knowing he was powerful. He demanded the respect that came with it, too. His hair was slicked back, but there was a wave to it. He wore an expensive dark suit, and if it wasn't for the soft look he gave whenever he was talking to Snow, he'd be scary. Snow wore a long shirt, jeans of some color, and sneakers. Total opposites in every way. Simon brought up the rear wearing clothes similar to Snow's. His hair was just as dark as his uncle's, but I had noticed his eyes were a lighter shade. There were many facial similarities to Christopher, but I suspected the ones I couldn't place belonged to Simon's mother who had passed of cancer when he was a baby.

"Good afternoon," I said as I stepped closer to them, hand out hoping Christopher would shake it. He didn't disappoint. "Hi, Simon."

Simon lifted his head, his gaze leaving his phone for a moment. "Hey, Poe. You have a nice house. I had no idea you lived so far away."

"No one did," Snow mumbled but smiled when I shot him a glare. "What?"

"It's necessary," I answered Simon, who shrugged.

"Pops says that whatever the reason means a long and dark

explanation." That earned him a light slap from Christopher and a chuckle.

"You go do what you're doing there." He gestured to Simon's phone.

When Atticus Spiros kidnapped Christopher and Simon, leaving Snow to help get them back, it was during that time, the bond between Christopher and Simon grew. It was also during that time, Snow learned the name of the Hart heir, even though he wasn't sure it was real. That horrific event secured the already strong bond they all had with each other.

"In a little while, Simon, I'd be happy to introduce you to Adelaide. Perhaps you two can find something to do."

Again, he shrugged, paying no mind to who Adelaide was, just going with the flow. He plopped himself on the chair on the far side of the room away from everyone. With ear buds in his ears, he got lost in the web.

Christopher then walked over to Phin. There was a note of understanding when Phin didn't rise to greet the man. No question, Snow prepared him for what he'd see when they met. After a beat of silence, he sat in the other wingback chair beside Phin's and held out his hand.

"Good afternoon, Mr. Hart. I'm Christopher Manos, you can call me Christopher. It's a pleasure to finally meet you." It was so proper and polite there was no hiding Phin's surprise.

"Good afternoon, Christopher. Please call me Phin." Slowly he lifted his arm and shook Christopher's hand.

"We should wait for the others before discussing anything. No reason to keep repeating ourselves. But we'll be here awhile. Poe." He rose and stood in front of me. "Since we have a few hours to kill before the room floods with people, I'd like to take this moment to personally thank you."

Okay, that was very unexpected. "What for?"

"I wasn't thrilled when Snow explained all this to me." He

swiped his hand in the air indicating the situation. "We spoke for a while about it, and in the end, I realized what you'd done."

He took a step back to include Phin in the conversation.

"You helped when it was asked of you, no question. You kept many of us out of jail numerous times, and I'm sure we'll never know the full extent of what you did. You protected Haven Hart repeatedly without an ounce of selfishness. In the end, if anything should happen to you, you've chosen me and Snow to guard the vaults. The secrets that have the power to decimate so many." He took a deep breath. "Being who I am, I understand how difficult the choices you've had to make are. You chose us for something outstanding."

He chuckled and looked over at Snow who had an expression of pure love on his face. "I realized last night you didn't do it to put a target on my back, you did it as an honor and out of respect. You knew if something happened, I'd protect Haven Hart with my life."

He was one hundred percent right. Often, I would have to hold back my emotions when dealing with Christopher or the others. It was becoming a difficult task. While I hoped someday to let my guard down completely, I had to be careful.

"A great amount of trust goes into this relationship, Christopher. It's something that must go both ways. I feel we have that and we should maintain it."

He nodded and we shook hands on whatever it was we were agreeing to.

Chapter Fifteen

Phin

Watching the interaction between Christopher and Poe was something else. Poe had become a force, and he was just as threatening as the crime boss who shook his hand. As time passed and each person arrived, I noticed they not only greatly respected Poe, they feared him in some way. Poe had made himself just as elusive as I was to them. Difference being, Poe had to face them regularly and hold the secrets close to his vest.

Everyone came up to me, making no mention of my not standing to greet them. Black was intimidating and quite large. His smile transformed his entire face, and his greeting was similar to Christopher's. Quill, his partner was, well, cute. He had dark hair and I chuckled at his rose-colored glasses. He wore a green long-sleeved shirt that just said Envy on it, and black jeans. He told Poe that when he wanted to come out, he came out like Miley Cyrus swinging on a wrecking ball. It was funny and while we laughed, I realized he was right. When we were done here, all these people would know everything.

Teddy and Riordan were next, and they brought their little girl Rosie. Teddy apologized profusely, saying the sitter ran off with some pool guy and no one told him. Riordan's family was out of town. Poe shut him down quickly, assuring him it was no problem, and Teddy then went around hugging everyone. Even me. I noticed he did this with each person who came in. Riordan just shook people's hands and grunted a greeting. He was a man of few words, but his body language spoke volumes. He placed a hand on Teddy's lower back, and oftentimes, kissed his daughter's head or made a silly face to make her giggle. He was stoic in the face of everyone in the room, but he adored Teddy and Rosie, and I could see why Poe chose them both.

When Bill and Mace came in, Christopher ribbed them good naturedly, telling them if they weren't lazy and had gotten out of bed sooner, they could've ridden in the chopper with him. Bill was a no-nonsense guy and shrugged it off. He shook Poe's hand and patted his shoulder. It was nice to see these people genuinely cared about my husband. Mace was a joker and said they'd been awake hours before but never left the bed. Bill rolled his eyes, and it was easy to see the dynamic in their relationship.

Christopher's security team, outside of Bill and Mace, were Frank and Donny. He didn't think it necessary to bring more. He mentioned another guy, Jerry, but explained that he wasn't one hundred percent since an encounter a few months back. When I asked what encounter, Poe explained he was hurt trying to protect Christopher and Simon. An RPG hit their caravan and Jerry got injured. Frank and Donny went with Tony to see the set-up in the security room.

The last to arrive were Lee, Jones, and Ginger. I'd heard a lot about Lee from Poe. He was a computer genius and likely the one who would be able to give us the most insight into the happenings of my family. Jones was almost as big as Black. A little shorter, bald, and like Bill, a man of few words. Lee greeted everyone with a hello, choosing not to shake hands. He spoke quietly to Poe for a moment then did, in fact, shake mine. He was a gorgeous Korean man, and I was aware he was a third in a relationship with Jones and Ginger. Ginger was all smiles when he stood in front of me.

"I am so freaking excited to meet you." He held out his hand, which I shook.

"Thank you, Ginger."

"Poe here is mister super-secret." He winked at Poe. I knew Ginger's story. Poe and I'd had a lot of catch-up conversations at night when everyone slept. Ginger had a very rough go with a man named Gregor Mims. Ginger was the one who'd taken him down, and knowing that man had been searching for Adelaide made me very grateful for him.

"He is that, but with good reason." I crooked my finger, and Ginger bent down closer to me. "Thank you so very much for all you endured, Ginger. You saved my daughter."

His eyes widened for a moment, but he righted himself and nodded. As soon as everyone had some refreshments and was comfortable, Poe began.

"Thank you all for coming here today. I know you'll tell me that you would've come sooner had you known, but let's pretend we went through that part of the conversation already and get to the meat of the matter."

Snow had done a perfect job of telling everyone everything up until this point. Who Adelaide was, that Poe and I were married, and I was in a coma for the last three years because my family tried to kill me. He did ask if anyone had any questions thus far and everyone shook their head. It was like they were afraid to talk or else Poe would decide not to continue.

"I've made these safeguards not just because I trust you all with such things but because Haven Hart matters to so many." He moved closer to me in a silent show of support. "I didn't keep Phin a secret because I wanted him all to myself. I did it because I had to." Gripping his hand, I spoke up for the first time.

"You all love someone, or even a few someone's, more than anything. You'd do what you have to in order to keep them safe. This is no different. And yet it's very different." Every eye in the room stared at Poe and me intently.

"Before my accident, I knew Poe was making friends. I'd

asked him to do it on purpose because I'd wanted him to be seen. When a face goes missing it's noticed. He then met Snow and Teddy. Every day he'd tell me about you guys. He never meant to make friends with people who could protect him, it was just luck. In the end, each of you had something in common. Haven Hart. You love it and you thrive there. You'll end it to save your own, but at the same time, you've suffered to keep it standing."

"Did you ever think of running? Leaving it to Christopher and Black to sort it all out on their own?" Quill asked.

"Sure," Poe answered. "But when Phin was in his accident, everything changed. I wanted to flee, but he always loved Haven Hart. His grandmother Camille was an amazing woman, and he wanted to keep Haven Hart the dream she'd created."

"But Haven Hart has been around for longer than your grandmother," Ginger said.

"It has. But it only really thrived under my great grandparents. Camille, she took the mighty spark Haven Hart was, and at the age of nineteen, made it everything. Her father adored her so much that before he died, he built the Camille Hotel in her honor. Made it more beautiful than any hotel he'd ever seen because she was his life."

"There's so much history here," Teddy said, his eyes filling with unshed tears. "Your family, Phin. You want to save the good parts and wash out the bad."

"That's what we've been doing, Poe and I, for years."

"And why now, with this ironclad plan, are you seeking to destroy the rest of your family when they can't touch you?" Jones asked.

"It's not that easy." Lee was the one to answer that. "Poe gave me this." He held up a flash drive. "He knew I'd find so much more than the maps to the city, isn't that right?"

"I did. But I also knew it was heavily encrypted. Only someone of your caliber could make sense of it."

"Flattery will get you everywhere with him," Ginger joked, and the room chuckled.

"Well, I was able to decrypt it, and I noticed many shifts in the programming. Some were a hell of a lot older than the three years you were in a coma." He slipped the flash drive in his pocket. "Poe, has in fact, secured Haven Hart in the event of his death, but what I was able to uncover was that someone hacked his systems."

"How badly?" Christopher asked.

"Enough that they not only discovered his after death plan, but they were able to find weaknesses in it." He held up his hand when the room started throwing questions his way. "Let me explain, Jesus."

"I suspected this," Poe said, finally taking a seat beside me.

"Poe was able to keep the Hart family back by promising he'd open the vaults to the public and all their dirty laundry would come tumbling out. That's a dangerous threat, but it's also one the Hart family took seriously. It's why they seemed to be quiet for so long. That, and obviously thinking they incapacitated you." He gestured toward me.

"Seemed? That's an ominous word in your sentence placement," Teddy said as he gave Rosie some juice.

"They haven't been as quiet as we all thought. They, too, hired some very smart people to help them get around a lot of Poe's defenses. While they couldn't interfere with his dealings, they were able to watch and learn. They were able to involve themselves in certain situations."

"Are you telling me they've been instrumental in things going to shit in Haven Hart?" Black spoke for the first time.

"I'm saying, while Poe put out a lot of fires and stopped a lot of issues, they were in fact trying, or at least helping others who were attempting, to get Christopher and Black out of the picture.

Before you even put the after-death clause together, befriending Snow and Christopher was terrifying to them."

Spikes of dread shot up my spine. My family was vicious. More so than I realized.

"Explain," Poe said.

"Trenton Hart," Lee said, and the name made my stomach turn. "My uncle."

"He seems to have taken the reins after your father passed away. Where your father was filled with anger over some of your choices, he downplayed a lot to the rest of your family. Naturally, when Trenton found out how much, he went into a spin."

"My father died shortly before…" I was interrupted by Mace.

"Yeah, your dad may have hated you and your choices, but not enough to kill you. Why would he have waited so long? Uncle Trenton is the one who was behind it all, isn't that right?" he asked Lee.

"Yes, but his father did try and assist Boris Sokolov years ago when they called on the Hart family for help. The Hart family was in business with Boris."

I wasn't aware of that. I knew from my own experiences that Boris Sokolov was killed by his son Roy, also known as Roman Sokolov. The same Roy who became obsessed with Snow and always seemed to be two steps ahead of Christopher.

"The reason the Sokolov's kept getting the upper hand on me was because of…"

"My father," I whispered in disbelief.

"It makes so much sense," Snow said, brows raised and a very nonchalant expression on his face. "Roy was an idiot and Boris didn't seem too sharp, either. Hearing this news actually fills some holes in that fuckery."

"You almost died," Christopher snapped.

"We all have almost died at some point." Snow pointed to

each of us. "And the Hart family probably had something to do with that. Am I right?" He was looking to Lee.

"Yes."

"Break it down for us, Lee," I said, and he sat on the stool by the bar in the room and began.

Chapter Sixteen

Poe

I knew as I listened to Lee that I should've retained his services sooner. I knew it was bad because, too often, I was righting disasters I suspected the Harts were causing. My own stubbornness and paranoia played a part in the waiting game.

"The battle with the Manos family was not new. For years the Harts tried to control them, before Christopher, but your father held them back, barely," Lee said to Christopher. "When you took the chair, it was almost hopeless. The Sokolov's already had a business arrangement with the Harts. They used the shipping crates and such and it was business, as I said. Until Snow came along, and the Harts saw Christopher had a weakness."

"But Roy tried to take Simon," Snow cut in.

"Coincidence. There was nothing around that time about Simon being used for anything on the Hart's side. However, when Zagan Marks came into play, it doesn't look like he had much push back from the Harts until Poe stepped in to help, then any Hart involved stepped back."

"And what about Black?" Riordan asked. "Emma, the mole?"

Lee nodded. "Yeah, not gonna lie, that was fucked up, and it does seem that while Emma didn't reach out to the Hart family directly, she got help from them, anyway. They used her and that entire thing to test the vulnerabilities of Black's business."

"What did they find?" Black was keeping his temper in check, but it was obvious by his glare that he was far from calm.

"Your father was never really on their radar because he didn't become rich because of the assassination business. It was low key. You were the one that made it thrive. And I hate to say it, Black, but you're the one that led the Hart family to the help they're getting today."

"What do you mean, Lee?" Black's voice dropped, and it dripped with anger.

"Calm down, big guy. Don't kill the messenger. You all need to know what we're dealing with and start realizing that they haven't been sitting on their hands all this time. They've been working around Poe's traps."

"If they realize Phin is awake and doing well, it'll be a disaster," I said, and the room exploded into conversation. It took a few minutes but everyone settled.

"I agree," Lee said. "Through Black, they were able to see his biggest competitors."

"Shit," Black whispered.

"Yeah, because they didn't just hire your top competitor, they snagged your top three."

"And who are your top three?" Teddy asked as he sat on the floor with Rosie and was building with some blocks.

"Talos, Menagerie, and Peluda." Black stood suddenly and walked toward the window. "Not real names of course, much like my own. But we're aware of each other. We had a mutual sort of respect. Never attacking the other." He began pacing, each step precise, and his stance reeked of agitation.

"Their organizations are successful, but not nearly as powerful as your own," Quill said as he stood in front of Black, halting his back and forth.

"But together, they can absolutely destroy me." He gripped Quill's shoulders and pulled him close.

"Black," Christopher spoke, and all heads turned in his direction. "The Hart family hired those three, your biggest competitors, why? Why not one or two?" The knowing smile that adorned his handsome face had me curious.

"Please, do tell us," I said as I sat back waiting.

"Alone, yeah, okay, maybe that's the end for you. But you're not alone." Christopher stood, came face to, well, nose with Black because he wasn't as big as the assassin. "Poe and Phin aren't alone. None of us are fucking alone!" He gave us all his attention now.

"Alone we can be defeated by this army the Hart family has been acquiring through the years. But together, there's not a chance. They wanted to destroy Poe and all the power he holds. Now they want to take us all out since we're the ones that will own it if he dies." He huffed. "I wonder, as they were all sitting around their shiny round table, if they thought all of us would be in a room together deciding to join forces to end them."

"Probably not," Bill said.

"Their plan, I'm almost positive, was to pick us off one at a time until just Poe was left standing. Then it would be over, and the reign of terror *Uncle* Trenton wants to have would begin. Because, let's not be foolish in thinking he's not the one making the calls, or possibly ordering them."

I knew Christopher was likely right. At the head of anything after the death of Phin's father, was Trenton Hart.

"Sweetheart," Snow said as he leaned forward in his seat. "If what you say is true, then we're more vulnerable apart."

He nodded. "We will be at some point." He walked over to Lee. "How long, by your guess, do we have until they start executing anything?"

Lee blew out a breath. "That's hard to tell. I agree with Poe, there's chatter so probably not long, but I'd say you have a month, maybe two."

"They'd have to organize and it would take time," I said.

"And they aren't aware Phin is not in a vegetative state," Riordan added.

"That is our saving grace right there." I squeezed Phin's hand,

and when my eyes met his, I saw tremendous guilt. "This isn't your fault."

"How can you say that? Everyone in this room has a huge target on their head because of my family."

Jones chuckled darkly. "Trust me when I tell you, a good percentage of the people in this room had targets on their heads already. Long before this mess."

"Can I say something?" Simon's voice almost shocked me. He'd been sitting so quietly all this time, I'd forgotten he was there.

"What is it?" Snow asked, a smile on his face.

"I was taken. Held against my will just because Christopher was my uncle. I didn't do anything to anyone and because we had the same blood, I was expendable. I was a weakness. I was something to hurt him with." He inched forward, closer to me and Phin, and I could see the man he would one day be. A man that would rival his uncle in many ways.

"Phin, you're doing this guilty by association thing. You can't. Pops' guy Jerry was hurt because we were taken. Should I feel guilty?"

"No," Phin whispered, clearly enamored by this brave thirteen-year-old boy.

"You fell in love with someone your family didn't like. You wanted great things for your family and Haven Hart. Because your vision doesn't fill your family's pockets enough, they want to kill it. Kill you. Kill everyone who tries to stop their greed." He shrugged. "Can't think of a better thing to fight for than love or keeping the good people alive in this town. And that's not on you to feel guilty about."

Phin smiled and nodded. "You're an amazing young man, Simon."

"Yeah, too true."

The room erupted in laughter, and Christopher patted Simon on the shoulder while Snow hugged him.

"Why don't we take a break," Teddy said.

"I'd like you to meet Adelaide," Phin said. "Poe, could you maybe go get her after we eat? Then, Simon, if you'd like to go hang around with her, I'd like that."

"Sure, sounds fun."

Sara brought in fresh food, drinks, and coffee. We spent the next hour eating and talking about mundane things; Teddy about his job and Rosie, Quill about his cat whose name kept changing as he spoke about her. He was happy that he was now the owner of three cats, much to Black's disdain.

Joey, Ginger's brother who was rescued from Gregor Mims' human trafficking ring a few months ago, was staying at Black and Quill's a majority of the time. Ginger was working through stuff, and they were rebuilding their relationship. Quill made a joke that Joey was cat sitting and how much fun it was having him around.

I was happy to see that outside this mess these guys all had lives. They were human above all else, and they were fierce in their loyalty. I had to believe we'd prevail.

"I'm going to go speak with Adelaide now since we're all fed and more relaxed. I'll be back soon so you can all meet her."

I left them in search for the girl of the hour.

Chapter Seventeen

Phin

I was exhausted. I felt it in my bones and everything. Even though I'd been awake over two weeks, it was a lot to take in. I wanted all their help and, in turn, I wanted to help them, but I was fading. Snow must've noticed because he walked over and placed a cup of coffee beside me.

"Are you allowed coffee?" he asked.

I shrugged because I didn't really know, but the doctor did keep spewing on about balance and watching what I ate. "One cup won't kill me."

"This is crazy, huh?" Snow was assessing the room. "How we're all here to stop a war, but we've been embroiled in it for years and didn't even know it."

"When I was a kid, Poe came to live with us. His folks worked for my parents. Nothing scandalous, they were staff. And one day, Poe was being bullied by these two shithead friends of mine. Not even friends really. My dad had colleagues and they were their kids. They were picking on Poe and I hated it, but it was the first time I got up the nerve to talk to him."

"By defending him?" There was a small smile playing on his lips.

"Yeah, so it's weird because I was grateful to have a reason and sad that's what it took to finally approach him."

"I stopped Simon from getting kidnapped, and in turn met Christopher. Weird beginnings make for fascinating adventures."

We were interrupted when the door to the grand room opened. Poe stepped in with a timid Adelaide. Her blue eyes flickered to all the faces. She had Countess Cocoa Puff in her arms and was using the kitten's tiny body to shield the lower part of her face. Adelaide had likely never seen so many people in this house at once and she was overwhelmed.

"Addy," I said, and her gaze locked with mine. "Come on over and I'll introduce you to everyone."

While she was eleven, brilliant, and sometimes wise beyond her years, it was social situations like this she suffered in.

She walked over to me as her eyes watched everything. Everyone smiled at her, and I knew they were doing their best to put her mind at ease. Poe followed behind her, his face stoic, a common tell I knew when he was trying to hide an emotion. Likely it was nervousness for Adelaide.

"Hey," I whispered when she was right next to me.

"Hey," she spoke into her kitten's fur. She was being so good and not even squirming. Her little paws were wrapped around Adelaide's wrist. Partners in crime, those two.

"I want you to meet some people who are very important, and you don't have to be afraid of them, okay?" She nodded. "This is Snow." I chose him first because he was sitting beside me.

"You were here the other day Tony said. Hi."

"Hello, Adelaide. It's wonderful to finally meet you. You look so much like your daddy."

She smiled at that, and it warmed my heart that she was proud to look like me.

I went around the room saving Simon for last. "This is Simon. He's Christopher's nephew and he lives with him and Snow. He's thirteen, a little older than you."

Simon walked over, and he was truly a tall boy. Adelaide was on the small side, so it made the difference really noticeable.

"Hi, Adelaide. This your cat?" She nodded. "I have a dog, Buck. He's a German Shepard and likes to drive Snow crazy."

She chuckled and it was just the thing the moment needed.

"And, Buck is a tramp and got the neighbor's dog pregnant,

and now we have all these little Germadoodles running around," Snow said.

"I thought you found them homes?" Teddy chimed in, and it started a back and forth that the room got involved in.

Adelaide watched in pure fascination as everyone started talking about the dog and the infamous Mrs. Markle that started a neighborhood uproar.

"I hear you like music." Simon was talking to Addy now, and she seemed more comfortable.

"I have a concert coming up and I've been practicing. Papa plays, too, more instruments than me." She pointed to Poe.

"Wow, that's awesome. I'd love to hear you play."

"Okay," Adelaide said. "Can Simon and I go to the music room?" she asked me.

"Absolutely. Show him all over if you'd like. Have fun."

"She's beautiful," Teddy said as soon as she and Simon left. "Riordan and I read your letter that you gave Snow. It's a great honor you're bestowing on us in the worst-case scenario. I promise we will all keep her safe, if the time arises."

I knew they all would. Poe spent years cultivating relationships with these people, and whilst they were all dangerous, they were so much more and they were here.

"Thank you."

The sun was long gone by the time we decided to end conversation for the night. Snow, Christopher, and Simon chose to fly back as did Black and Quill. Black explained he didn't want to leave Joey and the dreaded cats, but he also wanted to see what he could find on Talos, Menagerie, and Peluda. Teddy and Riordan opted to stay since it was so late and Rosie was cranky. I gave them one of the guest rooms, and they settled in for the night.

"If it's alright with you, I'd also like to stay," Lee said. "Jones and Ginger will be heading home and seeing how they can assist Black, but I'd like access to your home computer, if that's okay?"

I had no issue with it, but I deferred to Poe.

"I'll trust you with that, Lee. How long will you be staying?" Poe's arms rested in front of him, hands folded together. He wasn't wearing his glasses, and I was able to absorb his sharp long features. The angelic and placid expression he was giving Lee. His pale skin was flawless and his shiny dark hair was like silk. I wanted to be alone with him so badly.

"A day or two, and then I'll meet up with Black and see what I can connect. The deadline is two weeks. We can all meet back here and formulate a plan."

I nodded as Poe spoke up. "In the meantime, tighten security on Black's information. I'm not sure Christopher will—"

Lee cut him off, and the slight twitch in Poe's cheek was all the reaction of his annoyance I saw.

"I will contact Christopher's people as well as securing yours. Riordan and Teddy aren't going to be immediate targets, but they are vulnerable, so I'll set up security for them, as well."

Lee left shortly after. There was a couch in the office, and he said he'd prefer that so he could work and sleep in one place.

Bill and Mace left with Christopher, and when Jones and Ginger walked out the door, the house was blissfully quiet.

"I'm exhausted," I whispered, and Poe whipped around and crouched in front of me. The mask he wore around everyone else slipped free and the stunning, caring, protective man I loved more than my own life stared concerningly at me.

"Let me carry you to bed, love. It's been a long day, and there's so much we need to do." He pressed his lips to mine, and it was like a second wind rushed into me. Lifting my hand, I held the back of his head, keeping him there.

He chuckled against my lips. "We're going to have to really

talk to the physical therapist about getting you more mobile so you can wrap those legs around me, and I can fuck you against the wall."

Fucking hell. "Yes, please."

We kissed for a few more moments and as promised, Poe carried me to bed. I don't remember much else because sleep claimed me.

Chapter Eighteen

Poe

Lee was clicking away at the computer in my office by the time I made it downstairs. Phin was still asleep, and with his physical therapist not arriving for a few more hours, I left him to rest. He wanted to be worked hard. He felt he could walk because he could feel his legs. One thing about Phin I learned years ago was that no one could stop him if he wanted something bad enough.

"Good morning." I leaned against the doorframe to my office, two cups of steaming coffee in my hands. Lee's eyes immediately went to the mugs, and I put him out of his misery by handing one to him.

"I've been up for three hours, slept two. You have a lot of data here."

Nodding, I went to stand behind the office chair to glance at what Lee was currently looking at.

"This location is safer than anywhere in Haven Hart. I keep most of it here." I pointed to a case that leaned against the side of a bookshelf. "That laptop is synced to my computer. Before I leave here, I boot it up and sync them. Those two computers are the most informative."

Lee eyed the case, then me. "I don't suppose you'll let me take that laptop with me, would you?"

I trusted Lee, but with everything leaking through, I had to protect what I still could control. "I think it's best it stay on site here for now."

"Very well." He went back to typing, and I saw blueprints of abandoned buildings owned by companies. The ones in blue were legitimate. Many were renting for election campaign headquarters or used during Halloween to sell costumes and holiday supplies. The few in red were questionable. Owned by dubious corporations. When you followed their trail, you always hit a wall.

"Any luck figuring out who owns those buildings?"

He stopped typing and clicked over one. "Learning that the Hart family has retained the service of Talos, Menagerie, and Peluda, I'm assuming it's one of them. The Hart family can't back the sale due to the hold you have on all their decision making. I'm working to see if I can figure out which of the trio does, and if I can destroy the sale, or perhaps make the property unsafe, or suddenly"—he shrugged—"have it catch on fire, then that would be great. I just need to be one hundred percent sure."

I wanted to know more about these three assassins, but Lee needed to figure out that information. I left Lee to it and bumped into Sara on my way toward the security room.

"Morning." She smiled. "Breakfast will be in half an hour. Your guests are in the grand room having coffee." She was referring to Teddy, Riordan, and Rosie.

"Thank you, I'll join them shortly." I made my way to the security room.

Tony and three of his team, Logan, Angel, and Missy, were looking over the monitors intently.

"Anything I should concern myself with?" I asked, smirking when Tony jumped.

"Make some noise, Poe. Jesus."

"I live here," I joked.

"Video surveillance picked up some odd activity a half mile from the property," Missy, who was no nonsense all the time, said.

Any ounce of hilarity I found at startling Tony was gone with Missy's words. "What sort of activity?"

"We have cameras that are set to see over thirty-two hundred meters from the property. With them being half that distance, we should've been able to see faces, but they were covered up," Logan said.

"They? What activity?" My cheeks were getting warm, and I felt the shake of anger through my body. "Be vague with Adelaide, never with me. I want you to stop talking outside the box and jump the fuck in!" It wasn't often I lost my temper, but everything I held sacred was in this house. Having it threatened was not something I took lightly.

"Sorry," Missy said. "At one this morning, shortly after you all finally went to bed, there was a lone figure by the field over there." She pointed to empty land on the monitor. "Now I can't get eyes on where your friends' helicopters landed from our cameras, but Gina drove down there when we noticed the guy who was alone got a few more buddies. All coming from the direction of where your guests landed."

"Did Gina find anything?"

"Just a bunch of tire tracks," Tony said.

"The people in the field, are you able to get anything on them?"

Logan shook his head. "Nothing. They stood there a while, talked, two of them smoked and I watched, hoping they'd drop the cigarettes so I could grab them, but both pinched them and kept them."

"A regular person wouldn't do that, would they?" I said as I stared at the frozen image of four people completely covered. "And they sure as shit wouldn't be covered up like that."

"We're working on it," Missy said. "Lee told us this morning he wanted to up the security, so maybe if they try to come close again, we'll be able to get better images."

I was livid, and at the same time, terrificd. Of course, that much activity would draw attention. Big names leaving Haven Hart at once would be followed somehow. Finding out there were other assassins working for the Hart family made everything worse.

I entered the grand room with more force than I meant to, and Teddy jumped and said louder than I'm sure he intended, "Oh shiitake mushrooms, Poe, you scared the lollipops out of me."

I was so taken back by his words, I ended up laughing. It was also an uncommon thing for me. "What did you say?"

"Sorry." He shrugged. "I limit curse words around Rosie. Sometimes it makes me seem weird."

Riordan grabbed Teddy's hand and pulled him to his lap. "I love your kind of weird." Then they kissed and I wanted to leave. I went to do so, but Riordan's voice stopped me. "Before you run away from displays of feelings, care to tell us what had you storming in here?"

I sat and explained everything to them. Teddy was visibly worried, and Riordan seemed determined and assessing.

"Teddy and I have to return home today. I'll watch and see if we're being followed. We need to let everyone know they may be closer to all this than we originally thought."

I agreed, and when Sara announced breakfast was about ready, I excused myself to get Phin.

Patricia was in the bedroom assisting him, and he beamed when he saw me. "Hey."

"I was just coming up to take you to breakfast." I ran my fingers through his hair, loving the silky curls. "I like when your hair is this length."

"Then I'll keep it this length," he answered with adoration. I leaned down and kissed him a proper good morning. Patricia left and I enjoyed the moment.

He smelled of his earthy soap and tasted of mint. His skin was soft and his lips were firm. I could savor in length every part of him for hours as I tasted and caressed him, but he had to eat before therapy, and I just hoped later we'd have time to do more exploring.

"Riordan and Teddy are leaving after breakfast. Let's go down and I'll catch you up on the morning."

With one last kiss we parted, and I lifted him into my arms. He wasn't a small man, and before the accident, I wasn't sure I'd have been able to pick him up. It was a struggle now, and I knew once he started packing on some muscle, I wouldn't be able to do this.

At the breakfast table, Lee and Phin quickly caught up on the video surveillance, and Lee said he was going to expedite everything in the way of security right after he ate. Phin looked as worried as I felt, and I tried to reassure him with a squeeze of my hand.

We'd just finished eating when Patricia announced the arrival of Elliott, the physical therapist. He wheeled Phin away, and I said I'd be there in a short while.

Riordan and Teddy packed up, and as they left, Teddy hugged me and Riordan promised to be vigilant.

I only hoped we got ahead of this before it all came crashing down.

Chapter Nineteen

Phin

"I spoke with your doctor and all tests and scans are looking great. One thing we'd been worried about was something other than your legs stopping you from walking so that's good news." Elliott was rubbing my legs while he had me lifting four-pound weights. It was sad that by the fifth pump I was sweating.

"I feel everything," I said as I dropped the weight on the cushion beside me and grabbed the cup of water he offered.

"Exactly, so it's a matter of building your body up to be able to support yourself."

After I chugged the cup of water, he handed me the weight again. "I'd like you to do five more. And I heard you wanted to double your efforts in walking and strength?"

"My life is currently full of vulnerabilities; I need the ability of my legs." I pumped and breathed. Pumped and breathed.

"I appreciate that, I really do. But, here's the thing. Too fast, too soon could be bad as well." He took the rolling stool the doctor used often when he talked to me and sat on it. "But, I have some ideas of what you can do that won't stress your body."

I finished the weights and placed them next to me. "Please tell me."

"I noticed that the glass around your pool closes, making it possible to use longer. Weather and temperature won't be an issue. I recommend doing some exercises in there. We have equipment that will keep you afloat. Work on moving your legs and kicking. A pool is the best place for that. When I'm here with you, we will work on other exercises."

"Perfect!"

"Okay, next I'd like you to place your hands against mine and try and push me away."

Poe came in while I worked and watched. He got called away a few times but always came back. Adelaide and her kitten moseyed on in just as Elliott and I were finishing up.

"Great job today," Elliott said. "I'll leave instructions on the pool exercises with Patricia. You won't be seeing me tomorrow, but I'll be here the day after."

"Thanks, Elliott." We shook hands, and after he left, my two favorite people came over.

"You super strong yet, Daddy?" Adelaide sat beside me and smiled while Countess Cocoa Puff meowed from the floor.

"Not yet, but soon."

"Papa was going to come play music with me because after lunch Tony and Sara are going to take me outside and play hide and seek."

Hide and seek. Yeah, Poe had told me that Tony has been teaching her how to hide, and he said the point was to not let him find her. I knew while fun for Adelaide, the reason was so that if Tony or I or Poe yelled hide and seek she'd likely understand. At eleven, the novelty was wearing off, but it was our fun way of teaching her how to stay safe.

"I'd love to hear you both, then maybe after, Papa could help me shower. I worked up a sweat."

She chuckled and waited patiently while Poe helped me into the wheelchair. We passed Lee, who had papers strewn all over the office. He waved at Addy when she said hello but was deep in thought.

Adelaide's music teacher was sitting there waiting for us when we walked in. "Good afternoon," she said. "Adelaide wanted to play you one of the songs we will be performing at the concert. Now we don't have the entire orchestra but with Poe, myself, and Adelaide, we can do something amazing."

I smiled, excitement bubbling in my stomach. I loved listening to Poe play. I hadn't had a chance to really watch Addy since I woke, so this was going to be wonderful.

"What are you playing for me?"

Adelaide smiled. "A section of the concert is devoted to original scores from movies, and this one is called 'Day of the Dead.' It was in *Batman versus Superman: Dawn of Justice.*" She fist pumped the air and I burst out laughing.

"Have at it then."

Adelaide took her place on the bench, fingers on the keys, and the seriousness on her face made my eleven-year-old daughter appear twenty-five. The music teacher lifted her violin and rested it on her shoulder. Poe walked over to the electric piano and winked at me. "This gets the best effects," he said.

It was silent for a moment and then Poe gently played, and seconds later Adelaide joined, in perfect sync with him. It was so stunning tears filled my eyes. She was intently watching her papa, not the notes. She knew it. When the music teacher joined them, it was beyond impressive. The three of them made it sound like an entire orchestra was playing in our music room.

A minute later, Lee stepped in followed by other staff. The sounds calling to them. It was like they were pouring all their emotions into it. I felt it, I felt them, and tears flowed down my cheeks with every lift, dip, and purr.

When the last notes were played, silence descended. I could see Poe's eyes were glistening, and when Adelaide turned to face me, I opened my arms to her. Without a moment's thought, she ran into them.

"I am so proud of you," I whispered into her hair.

"I'm so happy you're awake." She sobbed and I just sat there and let her while everyone around us dispersed except for Poe.

"How about tomorrow, the three of us have a family day?" Poe said as he brushed his fingers through Addy's hair.

"What are we gonna do?" she asked as she lifted her head from my chest but stayed sitting on my lap.

"Well, maybe a movie, we can take a walk, it's going to be cloudy, so perhaps a picnic and then more music. Whatever the heck we want." Poe smiled and we both returned it.

"Great!"

A knock on the door grabbed our attention. Tony and Sara stood there.

"Hide and seek time." Adelaide jumped off my lap. "Have a good shower, Daddy," she hollered as she ran out of the room, Tony and Sara trailing after her.

"Let's get you cleaned up." Poe lifted me up so quickly I teetered and thought I'd fall.

"Careful."

"I'd never drop you," he whispered against my cheek. I knew he wouldn't. If I couldn't walk, than this was the next best thing. I enjoyed the closeness all the way to the bathroom.

Poe sat me on the small bench in the master bathroom. It was a remarkable room. There was a huge shower with four cascading jets. You could adjust the pressure to either massage or flow. I loved the flow because it was like standing under a calm stream. The walls were rocks, and they heated if it was cold and chilled when it was hot. The huge tub was oval and big enough for four. It was made of smooth rocks around it, but inside, not so much. No jagged things hitting my parts, thank you.

Poe walked over to the tub and began filling it.

"No shower, then?" I asked.

"I've decided to join you, and that's more fun in the bath."

Yes. I wanted that so fucking much. My cock perked up at the thought. "You, wet and naked. Absolutely."

He chuckled as he began stripping himself of his usual dark clothes. Black everywhere. It wasn't that Poe was a morbid person, he was someone who always wanted to hide. When he was put into the position he was in, by myself, hiding was something he couldn't always do. Clothes were his armor, and I wasn't going to change that.

"Your turn." He stood alabaster and beautiful before me. His skin pristine and his cock long and plump. There was no hiding how excited he was for this, too.

Chapter Twenty

Poe

With Phin's back to my chest, I leisurely washed his body. The scent of roses and sandalwood filled the bathroom, and as his fingers ran up and down my thighs, I felt overwhelmed with how fast everything went from adrift to anchored.

"I missed this," I said as I dipped the sponge into the water.

"You know, when I was in the coma, I heard you sometimes. I remember the music. It was frustrating and no one ever tells people that."

"Tells them what?" The stabbing sensation in my heart almost took my breath away. The paralyzing feeling he must've been enduring, *my god*.

"That it's not like no time has passed. I was mixed up all the time. I had no idea what was happening." He shifted, lifting himself a little using my legs for leverage. "It didn't feel like that always, I'm sure, but all I remember was wanting to answer the questions you were asking." He huffed. "I can't even remember them now."

It took some serious maneuvering, and water splashing on the floor, but I managed to turn Phin so he faced me. I pushed him to the other side of the tub, his back resting against it.

"What are you doing?" Phin chuckled.

"I'm trying to get your legs around my waist." Again, it was a minor struggle, but moments later, he was wrapped around me and I could look at his beautiful face.

"I'm told you have golden blond hair and piercing blue eyes. Adelaide said your skin is as white as mine, but when I compare us, the shading is off. My mother said when you were younger your mouth always looked like you'd eaten a ton of red candy." I smiled when he did, loving how entranced he was with my story. "I may only see in black and white, but I feel in color, Phin. I don't know what red or gold or blue look like to you, but to me you're a storm of gray, a contrast of white, and a calm of black. You're art I can never paint."

"Why are you telling me this?"

Tenderly, I rested my hand against his cheek, warmed when he leaned into it. "We were living the same nightmare and neither of us knew it."

There was an intense silence before Phin spoke, "I want you to take me to bed, Poe. Addy will be a while, and right now, I need to feel you."

"But…"

"No, I spoke to the doc. It's ok, just no reverse cowboy or anything."

I laughed with him but didn't want to argue anymore. I needed this, too. I reached behind him and hit the lever. The water began to drain and I untangled us.

"Let me get out, then I'll get you out and dried off before I ravage you." I never wanted Phin to feel like less because he wasn't at one hundred percent, and while he smiled at me, it was dimmed. He wouldn't always feel that helplessness, he'd gain his confidence.

I lifted him out of the tub and onto the fluffy towel that was opened on the toilet. After we were both dry, I carried him to bed.

His skin was slightly damp to the touch, and the quiver in his muscles as my fingers danced up his legs until I reached his chest had me hard in seconds. Who was I kidding? I'd been hard since I stepped foot into the bathroom.

"Kiss me," he pleaded, and there was no way I was denying him anything.

My lips only just whispered against his before he opened. Our tongues danced tentatively at first, then it was like all the years that held us back came rushing forward. It was all teeth, tongues, lips, and hungry moans.

He wrapped his arms around my neck, and I already felt some of his strength returning there. Using my knees, I spread his legs so I rested between them. We just kissed for a few wonderful minutes until the urge to taste more of him became overwhelming.

I ran my tongue down his throat, relishing in his salty taste, his clean scent, and the texture I'd been deprived of for three long years.

I loved Phin's incoherent mumbling as I went lower. I kissed or licked every inch I could until I reached his cock. Softly I blew against his glistening head, smiling when his cock twitched.

"He looks cold," I joked.

His closed eyes opened, and the lust that shone through left me breathless.

"Don't tease me, Poe."

I didn't want to tease him, I wanted to devour him. I licked his shaft from base to tip before I slid my lips over it and sucked. I knew he wasn't going to last long and I didn't care. He may have wanted to get fucked and I wanted that, too, but if he came in my mouth and passed out, I'd love that, too.

"Poe..." he repeated my name over and over again.

Gently I squeezed his balls, they were so tight and it wouldn't take much for him to come. I wanted this to last forever and at the same time, I needed to taste him almost as much as I needed air.

I lifted off and jacked my hand over his hard cock. "Come for me, baby."

Phin released a guttural moan and with so much passion said, "I want you inside me. I want to come with you inside me."

"It'll happen, but I want you to come for me now."

I was surprised when he arched his back up. I didn't think he could do it, and I wasn't even sure he knew it was happening. I wrapped my lips around him once more and sucked. A second later, his come was filling my mouth and I swallowed. Savoring every drop of him.

"Sweet Jesus." He was breathless and the sheen of sweat that shone off his skin made it look like he was glowing.

"You still taste amazing."

He peered down at me, a sated and mischievous smile lingered on his face. "I wanted you to fuck me."

"Oh, I'm going to do that."

He blinked a few times, each longer than the other.

"Now I'm exhausted. I want to suck you."

I chuckled as I crawled up his body, hovering over his face. "You want a lot."

"I want everything."

We kissed and I collapsed on top of him, face in the crook of his neck.

"I'll give you the world, Phin."

"You are my world." He pressed his lips against my hair and I just hummed.

The sounds of the house were muted in the cocoon we'd made. His fingers brushed against my skin. There was no more talk about fucking and wanting more. We had enough in each other.

I knew we only had an hour left before Adelaide would be back from hide and seek, so I closed my eyes and breathed in our mingled scent. I was still hard but it wasn't bothering me. I tasted Phin, I was breathing him in. Nothing in the world was going to ruin this moment.

Chapter Twenty-One

Phin

The next three weeks went by uneventfully. Lee had secured the house better, and no more lone figures or groups had been seen since. As far as research and such, everyone was still digging. Not wanting anyone to find us all in one place, we decided not to meet again right away. We did a lot of video conferences on equipment Lee supplied.

My physical therapy was going great, and with the help of a walker I was moving, slowly, but it was progress.

"Are you ready?" Adelaide asked for the tenth time in five minutes. It was the day of her concert, and we were all driving the thirty minutes to the music hall where it was being held. Her tutor knew who Addy was, but none of the kids or staff did. They thought her name was Amber, and she understood there were reasons for her protection.

Adelaide was wearing a beautiful rose gold colored dress, with shiny white shoes, and her hair was up and out of her face. A cascade of golden curls fell down her back, same color as mine. Every time I looked at her, I could never find any trace of her mother Pricilla. Her mother, when she was alive, was very beautiful. Caramel colored hair, dark eyes, and sharp features. But Adelaide had none of that.

"Yeah, let's go," I said as Tony held the door open for us.

Missy was there as added security and got in first, followed by Addy, then me and Poe. Tony was last and the five of us drove to the concert with Corey behind the wheel.

"It must be weird being here all this time, Corey," I said as he turned on the main road.

"It is. My wife and kids are thrilled, though."

He was always with Poe, but Poe hadn't gone back to Haven Hart since he'd found out I was awake. Instead, he'd been working from home.

"That's wonderful." We fell into a comfortable silence.

Adelaide was asking Missy why her tattoos were white and not black like those she'd seen.

"Well, you see how my skin is dark?" Addy nodded. "The white ink pops more on my skin."

"It's real pretty, Missy."

"Thanks, squirt."

We arrived at the concert hall and Tony stepped out first. I was slower than everyone else, but they were patient. I took the ramp up while Poe and Addy took the steps. At the top they waited for me.

"You have to go in the back, right?" I asked Addy.

"Yup."

I met Missy's gaze and she nodded. "I got her."

The two of them went inside and to the right, and we went in and straight into the auditorium.

The hall was stunning, my grandmother would've loved it. We sat in luxurious seats. Poe was to my right and Tony sat to my left by the aisle. The velvet curtain was closed, and I knew it would open to an orchestra. Adelaide was so immensely gifted that she was part of an elite musical group of children. I wouldn't be surprised if every child up there made a future in the music business.

The lights dimmed and the curtain opened. The conductor stood before the crowd, gave a warm greeting and explained they would be playing many instrumentals for us today. He talked some more and then finally turned to the orchestra. Adelaide was smack in the middle. She was gifted in both the violin and piano, and I smiled as she rested her chin on the violin, ready to play.

I saw the list of songs and made sure to listen to each one before the concert so I'd know which were which. A boy, maybe a little younger than Adelaide, sat at the piano. He began playing and I immediately recognized it as "Light of the Seven" by Ramin Djawadi. I was sure none of these kids had seen Game of Thrones, I'd only heard of it. But they played the gorgeous composition flawlessly.

When the song was over, he gestured to Adelaide and then to the piano. She placed the violin down and walked toward it. A single spotlight shone, drowning out the rest of the crowd.

She began playing her solo "Kiss The Rain," and I was fine one second and the next I was in tears. She was so amazing and she was mine.

Poe reached over and gripped my hand, almost too tightly, and even though he had his glasses on, I knew he was feeling it, too. I didn't need to see it.

When the concert ended, Adelaide came running down the hall, and Poe swept her up and spun her.

"You were brilliant, sweet girl," Poe cheered. He was so carefree in that moment it took my breath away.

She received many congratulations and Missy said how she was holding her breath backstage the whole time. "She's remarkable. You both should be proud," she said to us. And we were.

As we drove home, we all talked about what our favorite parts were and laughed when Adelaide said she beat out Rudy Naples for the "Kiss The Rain" solo.

We'd just pulled into the driveway when everything came to a screeching halt. The sound of shattering glass made us jump. The car jolted and it felt like it may have been a tire.

"Get down," Tony shouted. Adelaide screamed and I froze. Another sound of glass made me jump, and in an instant, Poe was covering me with his body.

"Don't move," he spoke into my ear. How was he so calm? I

saw Adelaide was also on the ground, Missy covering her. Tony was shouting into his mouthpiece, and I could tell it was very bad.

"Logan, come in. Angel, Gina?" He punched the seat just as a spray of bullets hit the car. Adelaide was hysterical and I didn't know what we were going to do.

"We need to move," Poe yelled.

"We don't have eyes out there," Tony said.

"I can make it to the garage," Corey shouted from the front seat.

"We have no idea if they're inside," I said.

"We have no choice. Do it," Tony ordered.

The car was in bad shape, and I knew Corey was risking his own life doing this. *Please don't let anyone die today.*

"I'm in," he yelled, and hit the garage door button.

We didn't move for a full minute, just listened. Then Poe reached into his jacket and pulled out his phone. Who the fuck was he calling?

"Black. They found us."

Tony started talking into his mouthpiece again, but there was no response. Slowly he opened the door.

"All of you stay here. Missy, be alert. I'm going to check things out."

"Got it," she said as she hugged a crying Adelaide.

"How soon can you get here? It's bad." Poe spoke into the phone and I listened. "We're in the garage. Tony went out to look. Black... Okay."

"What did he say?" I asked when he ended the call.

"Just that he's on the way. We have to hang tight."

Right.

Chapter Twenty-Two

Poe

Everything I loved. Everything I had protected for years was a bullet away from ending. I sat in that car, a prisoner in my own home without a clue how to keep them alive if the place was stormed. I jumped when the car door opened.

"We need to go. They're moving toward the house," Tony said.

"Who?" I asked.

"I don't know, just that there are ten I can see." He turned toward Missy and Adelaide and my heart ached. I knew the words he was about to say, and I'd hoped he'd never have to say them to my baby girl.

"Princess." Tony's voice was soft.

"Yeah?" she hiccupped.

"Time to play hide and seek." He met Missy's gaze. "Both of you."

"Tony, you can't—" Missy started to argue but was interrupted by Tony.

"She's your job. It's hide and seek time."

"Come with me, Missy. I know a great spot. They'll never find us." Adelaide grabbed Missy's hand, and then she kissed my and Phin's cheeks. "You guys will hide too, right?" Tears still flowed down her cheeks but there was no missing the brave front she was going for.

"Absolutely," I answered, and Phin nodded.

Tony moved out of the way and then Addy left. Before Missy exited the car, she turned to me and Phin. "With my life. I promise."

I couldn't speak. I knew Missy would die for Adelaide. In my heart I knew we'd lost people today, and I was trying to wrap my head around everything.

"Poe." Phin grabbed my face. "We need to hide until Black gets here, baby. Hide like Addy."

"Right."

"I'm too slow, I can wrap my legs around you. Carry me. Can you do that?"

Corey slipped out of the car and came around to the other door and opened it. "I'll help."

Tony stood by the door that entered the house. "Follow me, you understand? Don't stop for anything you see."

Phin was on my back and very heavy. Corey had our flank as we followed Tony. It was obvious right away that they were inside at some point. Tables were on their sides, and glass was everywhere. And what I assumed had to be blood was all over. There was so much. We passed a few bodies I didn't recognize, so they must've not been my own staff. I tripped on air when I saw Logan's body slumped to the floor. He sat in a pool of blood.

"Come on," Tony said as we went toward the basement. "There's a storage room Addy and I found. I told her it's a good size for her dads and she agreed. Get inside, all three of you, and I will latch it from the outside."

"What about you?" Phin asked.

"I'll hide in the basement. If anyone goes near that door, they'll wish they hadn't even tried. I'll be safe, I promise."

I wanted to argue, but there was a sound above us. "Addy?" I whispered.

"She's safe. She's smarter than all of us. Trust me, please, Poe." The pleading in Tony's voice had me moving. We climbed into the storage area, the three of us. He shut and latched the door. We waited. And waited. Somewhere in the house we could hear thumping and crashing.

"Why isn't Addy with us?" Phin said.

"If they find us, she won't be here," Corey said. "She can fit into places we can't go. This was smart actually." He seemed calm but his hands were shaking.

"I'm sorry, Corey." I placed my hand on his.

"No. Don't be. The Harts are doing this. Fuck them." He was venomous. I knew he didn't like them when he'd told me years before they'd worked his dad to death.

Phin was quiet. He rested against a wall, eyes forward and vacant. I hoped Addy was okay, but she was smart like Corey said. She'd hide in a ridiculously small place.

I had no idea how much time had passed, but suddenly there was a sound, almost like an explosion.

"What the fuck?" Corey whispered.

Sand and dust sprinkled down. We heard shouting, gunfire, it was like there was a stampede above us.

"Think they found Tony?" Phin asked.

"No. I bet anything Tony is still down here. He won't leave us for anything," I answered. More gunfire, thumping, shouting. No, it could only be one thing. "Black's here."

"You think?" Corey asked, hope shined in his eyes.

"He wasn't coming in quiet, not with that many people. He'd roll in like thunder and rain down holy hell."

Then there was nothing. Not a peep. Like everyone evaporated and it was just the three of us. When the sound of the latch being removed came, I leaned in front of Phin. When the door opened, it wasn't Tony's face I saw. It was Black's. His appearance was lethal. Dressed in dark colors, hair tied back, blood or dirt splattered his face and neck.

"You coming out or you want to stay in there longer?" He smiled, slightly jarring but relief washed over me.

Corey went out first, followed by Phin so we could help him. I was relieved when I stepped out and saw Tony standing there, a little worse for wear. Three bodies were at his feet.

"They never got near you," he said to me, and I never wanted to hug the man before, but I did now.

I gripped his shoulders and pulled his hulking body to me. "Thank you, Tony."

"Don't mention it."

"We have Adelaide," Black said as he walked past us and up the stairs.

I lifted Phin up and raced up the stairs as fast as I could. When we got to the top, I placed him down. Corey and I each took one of his arms and helped him as we followed Black to the grand room. It wasn't looking so grand anymore.

"Papa. Daddy," Adelaide shouted when we entered. I had to let go of Phin's arm to catch her as she jumped into my embrace.

"Sweet girl."

"You hid." She gripped me so tightly. I put her down and she gently hugged Phin. It was then I realized she was a mess. Her dress was torn, her hair had fallen out of her style. There were dark marks on the fabric. I hated my colorblindness right now.

"What is that?" I pointed to the stains. "Is it blood? I can't see, I don't know." I was frantic.

"Hey," Phin said. "It's dirt. Just dirt. Where'd you hide?" he asked her.

"Missy and I went through the back of the house, out the window in the music room to the shed. No one was there and we had made a hole a while back. We have a string you pull when you're in and an empty crate pulls over the hole."

Corey smiled. "That's brilliant. And you and Missy both fit?"

Silence again.

"No," she whispered. "I told her I had the string to pull, but she said get in there and put the crate over me. She…" She hiccupped. "She said she'd make sure no one came near my hiding spot."

Just like Tony. I met his gaze and the sorrow that shrouded his face told me everything I needed to know. Missy died saving Adelaide.

"I will destroy every single one of them," I growled, startling even myself.

Chapter Twenty-Three

Phin

The house was destroyed. Lee announced fourteen bodies. Fourteen. *Did my family hate me so much they'd go to all this trouble?* Yes. I was just an obstacle keeping them from the money and power.

"Hey," Ginger said, kneeling before me. "Got you some water."

"Thanks." I scanned the room. Adelaide had Countess Cocoa Puff on her lap. I was so happy we found her. She was huddled under Addy's bed shaking. But by the looks of it, she was happy now. Black and Poe were talking, and the intensity of their conversation had me asking Ginger what that was about.

"Yeah, seems they tried to hit Christopher and Snow's house at the same time as you guys. Black got a call from Christopher right before you."

"Are they all right there?" I asked as crippling dread shrouded me.

"Yeah. Black sent men over there. Jones leading the fray." He chuckled. "Christopher has his own army there. You guys weren't as protected."

"Do we know who hit them and who came in here?"

It was Lee who answered me. "Seems the men here are Talos', and Peluda went after Christopher."

"How'd you figure that out, smarty-pants?" Ginger poked Lee's arm making the stoic man grin.

"Talos' people have tattoos on their upper arms of Talus. Peluda's people all have a medallion of Peluda the French mythical creature."

"Not their real names, right?" I said. "What's Talus?"

Black's men were cleaning up the bodies, and they were all out of the room for Addy's sake, so he gestured for me to follow. With help from Ginger, I followed Lee to the foyer. Several bodies were in rows on the floor. Lee leaned down and lifted the sleeve of one of the guys.

It was an extremely detailed tattoo. It was human in appearance, but they used a bronze like ink.

"Talus was a giant automaton made of bronze and created to protect Europa in Crete from pirates and invaders. He'd walk the shores three times a day," Lee said.

"I know of Peluda. Hairy beast, hideous. These guys pick interesting mascots." I couldn't stay in the foyer anymore and slowly made my way back to the grand room. Ginger had located my spare walker, thank god.

"And Menagerie?" I heard Poe asking, obviously finding out the same information I was.

"They've been lowkey." Black turned toward me. "Peluda and Talos have numbers and they're lethal, as you can see. But Menagerie, they may be more worrisome."

"Why?" Tony asked as he came through the door, freshly cleaned and looking a lot better.

"Menagerie was created by a family. One man, his wife, and four daughters. The father ran it more politically. I used to deal with him, but a couple of years ago, he was killed. The wife and girls went quiet."

"They stopped killing?" I sat in the chair beside Poe, unable to stay on my feet.

"No, they were what we call underground mercenaries. Mysterious hits started happening out of nowhere. We didn't know where they were coming from. At one point, I even sat down with Talos and Peluda, and we decided to try and locate who was doing it."

A mother and her daughters were violent murderers? How is that a thing?

"It took Lee, of course, to find them. The mother wasn't well, but the daughters were still working, the oldest was running things. She made me a vow to never strike at me and my people without informing me I was a target."

"It makes you wonder what they, or she, is up to, huh?" Ginger asked.

"Not seeing her here today, you bet it does." Black took out his phone and was reading something.

"If you're friends, can't you contact Talos and Peluda and call this off? We can pay." The shake in my voice gave away my desperation.

"Friends?" Black huffed, eyes never leaving his phone. "This is business, not personal. They're my top three competitors. At the end of the day, being number one is what matters to them, Phin. They didn't target any of my locations, just Christopher and you. That's about as much respect as I'll get from them. Menagerie owes none of you anything and still wasn't here." His brow crinkled. "Lee."

Lee came over and Black handed him his phone. "Perhaps Menagerie wants to get in touch with you, after all." Lee took his phone and walked off.

"Is that them?" Poe watched Lee leave the room.

"Yes. He'll deal with it. Poe, you need to get in touch with Trenton Hart."

Poe's eyes widened and his cheeks turned red with rage. "To kill him?"

"No. It's time to talk, though. You, me, and Christopher. This ends somehow. I want to know the how of it."

I wanted to be there, and when Poe met my gaze he understood. "No, Phin. You can't be there."

"You think they don't know I'm awake and better, Poe? You

think all this was for you and a child they don't know?" Each syllable, my volume grew. "Nobody here can believe that."

"Phin." Poe's voice got lower, softer. "Even if you suspect someone knows you have a winning hand, you treat it like they don't. If there's even an inkling of doubt that you're better and we show up with you, we've given them something, and I don't want to give them a damn thing."

I knew he was right. It wasn't the first time he'd held me back when he knew if I intervened, I'd get hurt. I closed my eyes for a moment to breathe and remembered a time, long ago, when Poe came to my rescue with his calming words and perfect logic.

"And what are you going to do?" Poe asked. My leg was in a cast and I was stuck in bed after falling out of the treehouse.

When I came back inside, my father yelled at me and then blamed Poe for putting dangerous ideas in my head.

"He tore it down, Poe!"

He just shrugged. "And your idea is what? To hobble into his study and stare at him intently, Phin?" He took my hand. We were thirteen and fifteen, but it felt like we were old souls tethered together for decades. "Get better, then we'll build it again or maybe Corey will help us and some of the staff."

"He'll just take it down, again."

Poe chuckled. "And we keep rebuilding. Never let the bullies win, but be smart about it."

"Okay, Poe. I get it. But Addy and I can't stay here," I said after I shook myself from the memory.

"I have many safe houses. I don't know what Peluda, Talos, or

Menagerie know about those locations, though. Lee thinks your safest bet is to hole up in the penthouse in my office building. I have it there for emergencies. The chances of anyone getting up there are impossible."

"What about my staff?" I asked. I wasn't leaving them here defenseless.

"The casualties on your side, while upsetting, weren't high. You lost two security officers, Missy and Logan. Patricia wasn't here, nor was Sara, since they were given the night off. Corey was with you, and the rest of your security are intact. As you see, Tony, Gina, and Angel are with my people cleaning up."

"I want all my staff with me, then." I wasn't budging on this.

"Phin?" Corey's voice was timid.

"Hey, what's wrong?" He kept us alive. He gave so much to us, if he thought I wasn't going to ensure his family was safe, he was also nuts.

"I need to get home."

"Is that safe?" I asked Black.

"I don't think they have any eyes on Corey or his family. I'll send two men with you," he spoke to Corey. "If they have any signs that you or your family are in danger, you do as they say. Agreed?"

Corey nodded. "Yes. I just, I need to be with them."

"Don't explain yourself," Poe said. "If you're safe, that's what matters."

"If you need me, I'll…"

I was having none of that. "We'll call you when this shitshow is over."

He said his farewell and left. I watched as he walked out of the room and silently hoped he'd be safe.

Chapter Twenty-Four

Poe

When Adelaide came over to me and said she was exhausted, Black told me to gather everything I needed, and he'd make sure we got to the penthouse safely. Ginger and the others were staying to help clean up. Lee wanted to get all the intel transferred, so with weariness in my bones, I got everything together.

As we drove away from the only place that ever truly felt like home, my heart ached. The Hart family took this from me. From us.

Adelaide was passed out before we hit the highway. Countess Cocoa Puff curled up in her lap.

I was pulled from my daydream, remembering how only hours before we were listening to her music when Phin linked his hand with mine.

"I don't know how to do it," he whispered in the silence of the car.

"Do what?" I asked, bringing his hand to my lips and pressing a tender kiss to it.

"Be what my grandmother hoped I would."

I didn't think that was what he'd say, but the rush of empathy I had for him was heavy. "Baby, your grandmother knew you could do this."

"But I'm not, you are."

I inched closer to him. I'd straddle his lap if I could, but with Addy so close that was a bad idea. "They did that to you, Phin. They tried to kill you and couldn't. If your grandmother was still alive, she'd do what we're about to do and hunt them down to the end."

"If she was alive, we'd never be in this mess."

He was having a pity party, and while I understood his grief, there was no way I was attending.

"No. Stop it. If she was here, she'd be dead. Don't think for a second that's not true. But this, this guilt and blame you've decided to drown yourself in, ends. You have until we pull into the penthouse to get it gone. Hear me?"

The slight smile he gave me was enough to know a fight wasn't about to break out.

"Remember the night we got married?" he said, and the shock of the subject change must've shown on my face. "Just, bear with me."

I'd indulge him. "Go on."

"You said we had to consummate it, and I joked that we were totally doing that a million times and forever. Then I carried you into the house, slipped on the carpet, dropped you, and you broke your wrist?"

I laughed softly not to wake Addy. "Yes, oh my god, it was awful."

"Right, and we were in the emergency room, and I was pacing and apologizing, and you told me to get it all out now because when we got home there was going to be serious fucking, and you didn't want to deal with me crying during sex."

Tears filled my eyes as I silently laughed. "Whatever made you think of that?"

"You're always setting me right again. Always the anchor. Thank you."

"You may not realize it, Phin, but you do the same for me. You have many times. Just like in the hospital that night." I didn't let him rebut; instead, I leaned over, hand on his cheek to keep him in place and kissed him until we needed air.

It was two days later with Black, Phin, Christopher, and myself, all sitting around a table in Black's office, phone on speaker, that we called Trenton Hart.

"Don't speak, Phin. No matter how upset he makes you, even if he calls you out, understand?" Black said.

"I won't say a word."

I hit call and waited. There was a click and that voice that sounded so much like Phin, but gruffer.

"Good morning, Poe."

"Trent." He hated being called that, so naturally I was using it.

"What do I owe the pleasure of your time and call?"

"I want to arrange a meeting." Short and sweet. I wasn't giving him anything, yet.

His laugh was disdainful. "You own the world, Poe. You don't need my okay to barge in here and demand my company."

I watched the men at the table with me, none of them even flinched. No question they'd dealt with monsters before, maybe even worse than Trenton.

"I think we can agree that's not really an option anymore after your antics, Trent."

Silence. While I was sure Trenton knew about the attack, he also had a couple of days to be informed it failed. It must be killing him inside that I walked away.

"Antics?"

"Oh, we're doing that?" I chuckled. "Okay, fine, I'll dumb it down for you then." Black was rolling his eyes at this point. "You tried to kill me and what's mine, and then you thought it was smart to attack one of the most powerful crime bosses in the world and failed at that, too. Do you think anyone is going to let you go? Do you not realize the price on your head?"

"I don't know what you're talking about." He almost sounded

convincing, but he was breathing and there were words coming out of his mouth, so I knew better.

"I'm far smarter than you, and way more powerful. I dare say my army is more lethal than yours." Yeah, I was pushing him a little. I wanted him to snap.

"You aren't as smart as you think you are."

Across the table, Phin's hands were in fists. I'm sure his face was turning red, but to me he just appeared livid. I shook my head, hoping he'd keep quiet.

"I want a meeting, Trent."

"Who am I to stop you? You just said you had the power, He-Man." What I wouldn't give to punch this man.

"Give me a day and time and I'll pick the place."

"Because you don't trust me to make arrangements?" he asked.

"Not even a little."

He chuckled. "Fine, I'm not available until Friday. I'm taking Mallory away for a few days. I won't disappoint my wife."

"You're taking her away mid-week?" I asked. That was so strange.

"It's cheaper. Works better with the stipend you gave me."

We all knew Trenton was lying. He was buying time or something, and by the expressions on everyone's faces, it was obviously irritating.

"Fine. Friday at two. I'll let you know where. It will be me, Black, and Christopher."

"Now, hold on." He sounded angry; finally, a reaction. "You're bringing a crime boss and a murderer, and I suppose you want me to come alone?"

I had to laugh. I wanted to give him just enough to know I was well informed on what he'd been up to, but nothing about Phin.

"Of course not, Trent, I assumed you'd bring your buddies

Talos and Peluda." When he said nothing to that, likely stunned, I added, "You'll hear from me." I ended the call, and it was like no one in the room had breathed the entire time because there was a rush of air.

"Jesus," Phin said, breaking the moment. "He all but confirmed it all."

"We never needed his confirmation." Black stood and moved toward the mirror. "Menagerie called me last night."

"What did they say?" I asked. This was the first time he'd mentioned it since Lee took their call.

"Menagerie was retained to take me out. Peluda was for Manos, Talos for you. They confirmed that. In the end, they couldn't fulfill their side."

"Why? You said personal and business were separate, and that you not getting hit was as much respect as you'd get," I told him.

"I spoke with the eldest daughter, Robin. She said her father had rules. Things he swore by. He apparently respected how I ran things far more than I thought and promised to never go against me. They are honoring the deal."

"You didn't know?" Christopher asked.

"No."

"Why'd she agree to take the deal, then?" Phin asked, and it was the perfect question.

"She said she knew by taking it I'd live."

"But you have to know the fact the hit never happened that you're open to a new contract from elsewhere," Christopher argued.

"She's aware." Black didn't say anymore, and I was sure there was more to say, but Phin spoke up.

"I want to retain Menagerie," Phin said. "How can I do that?"

Chapter Twenty-Five

Phin

I heard what I said and I didn't understand why everyone was looking at me like I was insane. It seemed logical.

"Menagerie is going to have to lay low until the Harts are dealt with," Black said as he walked back over to the table. "You get what that means, right?"

I was fairly certain I did, and I had to take a moment. I thought about Trenton and how he was when I was a kid. He didn't seem so bad then. He bought me a baseball when my dad said it was a stupid game. He used to come into the theater room when I was by myself and keep me company.

"Phin?" Poe brushed his fingers against mine.

"Trenton wasn't always like this. I remember the good in him."

His smile was so sad.

"He's either no longer the man you're thinking of or he never was." Poe inched closer and brought his face to mine, dark eyes that sparkled when he looked only at me.

"I overheard an argument in your house. Many times I hid in the pantry because I'd steal the sourdough and jam you liked." I chuckled at the memory of him sneaking into my room with them. "I remember listening to your father fight with Trenton. Your dad wasn't a nice man, but he loved you in his weird way. Trenton wanted to push you away from the business while your father wanted you in it. I think he hoped he'd win, and your father would pass it all to him."

"But it wasn't my father's choice."

"I don't think he understood how ironclad your grandmother

made things." He squeezed my hand. "Sometimes we play the long game, babe, and I think Trenton was doing that to you. Hedging his bets. He wanted on your good side, but that didn't work, and when your father died, he tried to take it. Just like he's doing now."

I knew when I said I wanted Menagerie what it meant. And this was my family, my blood, but they wanted to wipe me away like I was nothing.

"You're going to kill him?" I asked Black and Christopher.

"I can't answer for Black, but I'll tell you this, and it's only out of respect for you I'm even giving you this much." Christopher stepped forward, and he was every bit the intimidating crime boss the world knew him to be. "He came after me and mine. I've killed someone for just touching my nephew before. Peluda came into my home, tried to kill me, my husband, my nephew, and even my fucking dog. It doesn't matter what you want, Phin. Trenton Hart will die. And any other Hart that had anything to do with this."

I closed my eyes for just a moment and remembered Missy's last words to me and Poe before saving Adelaide.

"Then we do what we have to."

"And you understand what you're saying?" Black asked.

"I'm not a fucking idiot, Black. I get it. You and Christopher are going to wipe out my entire family, right?"

"If they're all involved, yes."

"Then, yes, I get it." I stood, glad when my legs didn't give way and slowly made it toward the door. "I have to go lay down."

I wished I could make a big exit by rushing out and slamming the door, but I had to take it slow. I wasn't at one hundred percent. I felt Poe take my arm.

"I'll come with you."

"I'm fine. You probably have to be in the know for all of this." I jerked my head toward the room I just left.

"No, they have things to do. I think you need me more than they do."

We had just made it to the elevator when it opened and Quill stepped out.

"Hey, all done for the day?" His smile fell. I probably looked like shit. "Did Black piss you off? I can withhold sex from him for a day. I can't promise more. I'm not strong enough for that."

That made me chuckle. "No, he didn't piss me off. Just made me realize things."

He nodded and his gaze went over my shoulder. "He has an incredible ability to do that. It's hard when he makes you face the mirror."

"I just see demons."

He took a step toward me, and he never appeared more serious than he did in this moment. "If you're trying to see your reflection, but all you see are demons, then something is stopping you. Something that shouldn't be there. It's going to be hard and it's gonna hurt a lot, but you have to beat them down and find yourself."

He didn't say anymore, he just moved past us, likely to go to Black. We stepped into the elevator. "He's pretty smart," I said and Poe hummed.

"He's been through a lot. Too much. He learned and spent most of his life beating down his own demons."

"Black helped him, though?"

Poe angled his body my way. "It's what he does, Phin. Quill's brother was killed by Black. His brother, and Quill knows that. He lost his whole family. His brother was all he had left, and because of how he hurt Quill, Black did what he had to do."

"I get it. They'll never stop. Not until we're all dead. I just never did anything to any of them."

"No, you didn't." Poe pulled me to him, his smell wrapped

around me, same as his arms. "I pissed them off because that's what your grandmother wanted."

We both laughed and when the elevator opened to the penthouse, I felt a little better seeing Adelaide on the carpet playing with Countess Cocoa Puff.

"Hey, sweet girl," Poe said as he moved toward her. She gave him a hug and then me.

"Countess Cocoa Puff learned how to climb curtains today."

"What?" I looked over to the huge floor to ceiling windows and sure enough, through the light, were tiny claw marks.

"Yeah, she was fast too and I couldn't get her. Tony found a step stool. But it didn't work. Then she meowed because she got scared, and then Sara got the broom."

"Why the broom?" Poe asked.

"Why not the broom?" Adelaide shrugged. "She jumped on it, but it wasn't steady, and then she fell into Tony's hair. He screams really loud."

How were we not informed of any of this?

"Then some men came running in because I think they thought we were dying. But it was just Countess Cocoa Puff, so they left Tony to fight her off."

Poe burst out laughing and it was contagious, and a second later, we were all in hysterics.

"Is Tony okay?" I asked between bouts of laughter.

"Sara stopped his head from bleeding. He was so dramatic, Daddy."

Cat claws were vicious, so I didn't think he was being dramatic at all. That and their teeth were extremely sharp.

"And the Countess?" Poe reached down and scooped her up.

"She hid for hours after that. But she's okay now."

It felt amazing to laugh and, in that moment, while the three—well, four of us were blissfully happy, I accepted and understood why Trenton and any of the other people in my family who did this had to go. I didn't want to lose things like these stories about crazy cats, and I couldn't live without these two people.

"You okay?" Poe asked as he handed the cat back to Addy.

"Yeah, but I'm going to rest for a little bit. Call me for dinner?"

He gave me a far too quick kiss. "Want me to come with you?"

"Later," I purred. "Stay with Addy."

Slowly, I made it to the bedroom. I toed off my shoes and fell back on the bed. I fell right to sleep.

Chapter Twenty-Six

Poe

"So, when I was kidnapped and at the airport and all those cops came, and there was so much going on there was no way they wouldn't investigate, you stopped that?" Snow was sitting across from me in the living room. Phin was still resting and he decided to surprise me, but it turned into a million questions.

"Yes."

"So the P. Hart on the letter to the police chief was you?"

"Yes and no." I loved when Snow got annoyed. He always narrowed his eyes, huffed, and did the thing where his arms and legs wiggle... even when he was sitting down.

"Seriously? Come on, tell me the things!"

I chuckled. "I am married to Phin, legally, but never used his name. I go by Edgars, mostly. I have aliases and use many variations of my name; it keeps people unawares. The chief of police, like many of you, think the Hart heir is agoraphobic, or hiding, or whatever the rumor floating at the time may be. So, P. Hart he'd think would be the Hart heir, and fear won't let him question it."

His brows rose, there it was, that realization he'd thought of something. "Okay, so, if the police fear you and the FBI bends to your will, why aren't you siccing them on Phin's uncle?"

There it was. I did wonder when someone would ask it. Perhaps Christopher and Black just never thought to or they hated authority so much it wasn't an option.

"To let law enforcement know there was an internal war with the Hart family would show a weakness they'd jump on. The vaults hold so much information they often need, or in some cases often want, but it's hidden. If they, for once, thought they could get on either side of the dispute, it would cause greater issues."

"And you think Phin's uncle wouldn't want them to cause more chaos?"

I shrugged, because I did wonder if he would. "I honestly am not sure what Trenton will do in desperation. But he'd be foolish to try."

Snow took a sip of his coffee, eyes intently on mine. "Tell me, Poe, what are in those vaults that are stopping you from just opening them up? Would it hurt everyone or just the Hart family?"

I rested my mug on the round table and leaned closer to Snow. "You know not what you ask, Snow. You know better than anyone that once something is known it can never be forgotten."

"I do. I also know the power it has."

"To answer your question, the vaults will cripple Haven Hart if opened. The Manos name will have no secrets, Black's organization will suffer, and yes, it would kill Phin's uncle in every sense but the physical, but the sacrifice is too great."

"People are dying, Poe!" He stood and angrily paced. "You don't want to hurt me, or any of us helping you. I understand that and love you for it. Yeah, I said love." My shock must've shown on my face to make him repeat that. "So, I propose something huge."

"Oh. God."

He laughed at my obvious worry over his idea. "Let us in. Let us see."

"How does that help?"

Huffing, he came closer to me. "I can remember everything. Let us in and gather all the things that can hurt Christopher and Black's organizations. Then open them."

I appreciated what he was saying, and I did think about it at one point, but he wasn't understanding. "You may think I'm being greedy, maybe unfair, but I can't do that." I held my hand up when he was about to interrupt. "I'll explain. Christopher has done many illegal things, just as Black has. But they did it for a purpose. It kept the balance. Yeah, that word again."

He chuckled because it was true. The Hart family did thrive on it, just not all the Harts agreed.

"The information locked in there keeps the authorities from busting down Christopher's door or Black's, or Lee's or Jones' or…"

"I get it, go on." He gave me the get-on-with-it gesture.

"The vaults keep everyone in check. It's not a punishment, it's a leash for those who threaten the balance."

Phin walked in at that moment and smiled at Snow. "It's good to see you, Snow. I'm so sorry about what happened at your home."

Snow smiled and moved to sit back on the couch. "I live the life I do expecting anything. I appreciate your concern, but this wasn't your fault."

Phin's pinched expression gave away how he felt. He harbored guilt and no one was going to change it.

"So, what brings you here?" he asked as he took the seat beside me.

"I was really just coming to say hello, but I also came to tell you that Christopher will be wearing an earpiece on Friday when they go to see Trenton Hart. I'll be listening in since I can remember everything, and I wanted to see if you wanted to join me?" he said as he turned to Phin. I knew he was upset about not being able to go, for obvious reasons, but this was a nice thing Snow was doing.

"That would be wonderful." Phin smiled and I knew it made him feel involved.

"Great. I'll come here and Lee is setting it up. It's really perfect you're listening," Snow added, and Phin cocked his head. I admitted to being curious myself.

"Why?"

"Because no one knows the Harts like you do. If Trenton says something out of the norm or whatever, who better to know if it's a lie than you?"

And just like that, Snow gave Phin importance and a purpose.

"Brilliant," I said, and Snow smiled.

"I can do that. Yeah." The excitement was radiating off of Phin. Odd given the dire nature of the situation, but he needed to feel a part of this.

"Of course, you can." Snow stood just then. "Well, Christopher has me on curfew." He rolled his eyes. "I'll see you Friday." He waved and was gone so fast I didn't even get to say goodbye.

"Sorry I slept so long," Phin said as I got up to pour him some coffee.

"It was only two hours. I was thinking …" I trailed off.

"About what?" he chuckled.

"I'm taking you on a date. Dinner and everything."

I turned, mug in hand, and froze at the look on his face. It wasn't happiness.

"Are you insane? We can't go out! People are trying to kill us!"

I placed the mug down in front of him and sat. "Yes, that's why the date is on the rooftop." I pointed to the ceiling. "I arranged something."

The stark look of terror Phin bore melted to warmth and happiness. "I love that, Poe."

I leaned in and he met me halfway. We kissed for a few moments, my body reacting to his feel and taste. When we pulled away, we were both breathing hard.

"We'll have sex under the stars, my love," I spoke against his damp lips.

"I can't wait."

Chapter Twenty-Seven

Poe

It was a perfect autumn night. Halloween was fast approaching, and I knew Adelaide would want to go trick or treating. As I set up the pillows on the huge lounger Black had arranged, I remembered one particular year Phin and I went trick or treating. He was dressed up as a decaying vampire zombie thing—his words—and I was some heroic slayer. It was just the two of us. One of his father's drivers took us around, and afterwards, we camped out in Phin's treehouse. Hyped up on too much candy, we laughed until the sun began to rise. It was one of my fondest memories.

Quill had helped me set up gorgeous twinkle lights around a beautiful canopy Black had up here. I could tell he enjoyed this roof often, and I was glad for that.

With pillows, blankets, lights, and delicious food prepared by Sara, I was ready to go get Phin for our date.

I found him sitting beside Adelaide on the piano bench in the living room. Black had one delivered for her so she could play, and when I offered to pay, he said it was more a gift for him than her since her music gave the place some soul.

I chuckled as I realized they were playing "Heart and Soul" followed by "Chopsticks." Phin wasn't musically inclined, but Adelaide sat there with him, and I could tell by the huge smile on both their faces, they loved the moment.

"Pardon," I said when they stopped. They gave me their attention in unison, and it was when they were side by side the similarities were striking.

"Hey, Papa. Daddy and I were playing on the piano. Wanna play?"

"Perhaps tomorrow? I'm taking Daddy on a rooftop date."

She chuckled and Phin, very slowly, stood and made his way toward me. When he was beside me, he took my hand and smiled softly.

"I'm excited." He squeezed my hand and I felt that same joy.

"What am I going to do?" Adelaide pouted, but she wasn't truly upset, that was obvious.

"Sara and Patricia are over, and I heard you were all doing nails and watching movies and…"

"Oh." She bounced off the bench and ran out of the room without even a goodbye.

"I guess we're not worth fighting over." Phin laughed.

"Meh, win some lose some." I led him to the elevator that would take us to the roof. We moved at a slow pace, but there was confidence building in Phin and his steps were surer.

We rode up in silence and I realized I was nervous. Excited for sure, but also nervous. It had been so long since the two of us went on a date. Longer since we had sex. And both were happening tonight.

"Wow," Phin's reaction was breathless as the doors opened revealing the setup for our evening.

"Quill gave me a hand. Stringing the lights was tricky." I chuckled and together we moved toward the lounger. "Have a seat. I have food and of course…" I winked and hit a button on the small remote. Black had speakers on the roof, and a moment later, soft classical music played. "Music."

"This is so beautiful, Poe, thank you."

"I'd love to take you out on the town, but this is the best I could do for you." I lifted a lid that had Sara's homemade ginger chicken, steamed broccoli, and cheddar potatoes. All favorites of Phin's.

"Nah, once in a while those sorts of dates can be fun, but I much rather have ones like this. Where I have your undivided attention and we're comfortable."

I nodded. Neither one of us were ever partiers, and we favored staying in whenever we could, even as kids.

"I'm starving." He lifted his fork to eat and stopped to look at me. "Aren't you eating?" I was standing in front of him, frozen, my own food across the small table.

"Yeah I just… I just can't believe you're here sometimes. I always saw you and spoke to you, but it was like you were gone. And now." I huffed. "You're real and here and I can listen to your voice, see your smiles, feel your fingers squeeze mine in return."

"It's a lot, I know." He reached up and I took his hand. "Sit, eat with me, then make love to me under the stars like you promised. I want this tonight. We'll have plenty of time to focus on what comes next and what was."

He was right. I sat and we were quiet while we ate. Both hungry and slaves to Sara's cooking. Halfway through, we talked about Halloween and what we were going to do for Adelaide since going out wasn't a great idea.

"I was speaking with Black's assistant, Lana? I think that's her name. She suggested a party at the penthouse. Simon, Joey, she said some girl named Deena could come, and little Rosie? What do you think about that?"

I had to smile at the idea, it was perfect. "That's fabulous. Do you want to handle that?"

His eyes twinkled as they met my gaze. "I'd love to."

Some people took for granted relying on a spouse. I probably did before Phin's accident, but never again. It felt good asking him to deal with it and not having to.

When we were both full, I placed our dishes on the small rolling cart and moved them by the door. Phin had his head turned up toward the sky, and his grin sparkled like the stars.

"You're so beautiful." I hadn't meant to say it out loud, but when he turned that beauty my way, I was glad I did.

"Lay with me." He held out his hand and I went to him. The sky was clear and the air fresh and cool. I pulled the blanket over the top of us, and for the longest time we cuddled, looked at the stars, and listened to soft music.

Phin shifted beside me, and it took but a minute to realize he was trying to straddle me. I wouldn't stop him or help unless he asked me to. He grunted and it took longer than it would take most people, but then there he was, legs on either side of me staring into my eyes, the stars a backdrop for the moment.

"Hey," I said as I lightly pressed my hands to his chest.

"I'll have you know, I asked Elliott to help me do this." He laughed when my brows shot up. "I didn't practice on him, idiot."

"Good."

He placed his hands on both sides of my head and bent to kiss me. I knew he had to be working so hard, and I really didn't want him wearing himself out. Well, not like this anyway. His lips against mine were chilled by the air. I breathed in the autumn aromas and tantalizing smell that was Phin.

Wrapping my arms around him, I spun us and in an instant, I straddled above him. Phin safe in my arms, and our chests pressed together.

"I'm going to make love to you, Phineas Hart."

"You better Raven Poe Edgars Hart…" His brow furrowed. "Is there an Allan in there?"

I smiled. "No, I just use it sometimes. It fucks with people."

He laughed into our next kiss, but soon enough we were breathless, desperately removing each other's clothes. Needing to feel flesh on flesh, fire on fire.

The coolness of the night didn't bother us. It caressed our overheated bodies as we writhed against each other. When we were naked and entwined, I lifted my head to peer into his eyes.

"You're mine," I whispered to him.
"And you're mine."

Chapter Twenty-Eight

Phin

Feeling Poe's arousal against my leg, and my own hardening length, made we wonder if I'd even last longer than a minute. This man, my savior, the love of my life, my everything, stood by me when he had every reason to believe I'd never waken to him. Never laugh or love with him again. He took every blow my family threw his way, went shoulder to shoulder with assassins and mob bosses to guard Haven Hart, and almost died to keep Adelaide and me safe. That was hotter to me than anything. And he was mine.

"I really need to feel you," I said, and he brought his face to mine. Silky strands of hair tickled my skin, his fingers brushed over my chest, and when he spread my legs out to rest between them, I thought I'd cry in happy frustration.

He slid an arm free and reached over to a circular table and retrieved a small bottle of lube. "You'll feel all of me, Phin."

I didn't know if I shouted the, "Yes," out loud or in my head, but Poe chuckled. He sat up enough to squirt some lube onto his fingers. His gaze never left mine as he brought his hand down between our legs, or when his finger pressed against my hole. I arched up when the digit pushed inside me and tried to not look away, but my eyes rolled back when he hit my prostate.

"Fuck, Poe, oh my…"

His lips whispered against my exposed neck and a second finger joined the first. He pumped slowly at first, but when I started fucking myself against them, he added a third and moved faster.

"I'm going to come."

"You'll come on my cock." Poe's voice was rough, and when he slipped his fingers out of me, I whimpered at the loss. "Poe."

"I got you," he said, and a second later, I felt the head of his slick cock sliding into me. Gently.

This wasn't fucking, it was making love. It was breaking the seal that had solidified over our lives for three years. This was yearning unleashed. Once he was all the way in, I was able to wrap my legs around his waist.

"I can do this now." My voice shook as I held on to him and tried not to come that second.

"You're a miracle, Phin." He thrust into me, and any response was lost in the feel of us, together.

I gripped his back as his hip thrusts turned into long pulls, and soon he was slamming into me as we were chasing our bliss, like it would complete us.

"You feel so good," he grunted into my ear. I wanted to answer, but I couldn't. Tears fell from my eyes I was so overtaken by the moment.

We were completely wrapped in each other, just Poe's hips moving as he brought us to our climax, and he did. With a roar, I felt him come inside me and it spurred my own orgasm.

It felt like aftershocks when we began to come down from the high. Jolts of pleasure sparked through my body as he twisted into a comfortable position, his cock still inside me. He began to soften but still didn't move, and I didn't want him to, either.

"I could lay here forever," Poe said, echoing my own thoughts. I tightened my hold, silently agreeing with him.

We stayed late into the night, only to go back inside when the autumn chill became too much. Adelaide had gone to bed long before, and Patricia left a note at our bedside that she had zonked out watching TV and not to worry.

We stumbled into bed and passed out, only to wake to the sound of voices outside our bedroom hours later. The clock read nine, and by the sun gleaming through the tinted windows, it was morning. I had trouble sometimes deciphering time, but it was getting easier.

"Do you hear that?" I nudged Poe who grunted. "Poe, voices, should we go see what that's about?"

"Are they knocking at our door yelling fire, or run, or oh god no?" I chuckled out a no in response. "Then wait until…" And then there was a knock. "Fuck."

We were both covered, minus our chests, so I yelled to come in. Tony stood there with an apologetic expression.

"I'm sorry to bother you both. I know you were hoping to sleep in this morning."

"It's okay, Tony, what's up?" I sat up and Poe started to move. He was on his stomach, and the only effort he gave was looking over his shoulder at Tony.

"There are people here. Apparently with Friday now a day closer…" He paused to roll his eyes. "Everyone wants to discuss the plan."

"Now?" Poe finally turned enough to face Tony.

"That seems to be what's happening out there."

I nodded. "I can go out there, take your time, Poe."

"Who's there?" He asked what I didn't even think to.

"Lee, Black, Christopher, Snow…"

Poe waved his hand. "Okay, I get it." He looked over to me with smiling eyes. "I liked it when they didn't know where to find me."

I gave him a quick kiss, and as fast as I was able, began

getting ready for the day. I was halfway through my shower when he joined me. I couldn't resist washing his hair, and while it took me longer and I wasn't able to do it as well as I hoped, he thanked me and returned the favor.

By the time we stepped out of the bedroom and into the living room, it had been transformed into what could only be described as a control room at NASA.

"Why are you doing this in here?" Poe asked as he made a beeline for the coffee cart. "Don't you have a multi-million dollar setup just below us?"

"Yes, but we're no longer secure in the knowledge that everyone is trustworthy," Black said. "Knowing the Harts had a hand in helping Emma try and destroy my organization makes me question everything."

That made sense to me. Emma was an assassin in Black's organization. She became greedy and bitter and tried to take him down. It failed, but Teddy had almost died when she'd poisoned him with penicillin which he was highly allergic to. Then Black had to restructure his entire company. It was shortly after that I had my accident.

"Very well," Poe said and came over to me with a steaming mug. "Where's Addy?" he asked anyone.

"I brought Simon, so she's with him in her room. He was going to teach her video games," Christopher said.

"You gotta get Teddy over here if you want the best of the best," Black said with a laugh. Teddy was also a beta tester and reviewer for video games when he wasn't professionally hugging people.

"He'll be here later," Lee said. "I asked for Riordan to come by. He has his own security agency, and I began wondering if we could use his business for things instead of yours. Nothing I've found has Trenton Hart targeting Riordan and Teddy."

"That's a great idea," I said as I watched them all buzz around while I drank my coffee. It was a circus in here, but as terrifying as everything was at this moment, it felt nice to have friends and see the best of Haven Hart come together to fight those who wanted to change it.

Chapter Twenty-Nine

Poe

We all went over the plan for Friday; it took three hours, a lot of coffee, and cussing. Snow went into Adelaide's room with Teddy once he arrived to see about the video games. Once everything was solid, Black asked if he could speak.

"This morning, a worldwide contract got offered. Now, I don't think Trenton Hart wanted my organization to get it, but I would've found out soon enough." He nodded to Lee who clicked something on his computer, and the screen he put in place to watch the Hart meeting on Friday flashed.

"This is the contract. It's fairly simple. It's calling for the complete extinction of Menagerie. That's five hits."

"We were afraid of this," I said, and then I saw the amount. "How is he planning on getting his hands on fifty million dollars?"

"That's what shocked me. Not the hit. He's on an allowance, right?" Black asked as Lee shut the screen off.

"Yes, and since the shooting I've frozen his accounts."

"You have?" Phin asked.

"I wasn't giving him money to feed his attacks. Of course, I did."

"Which tells me he's planning on getting his hands on that kind of money, somehow." Phin sighed, the exhaustion of this whole thing was getting to everyone.

"He must think he's killing us all then." Lee huffed. "You die we get it..." His voice trailed off and he began typing away.

"What is it?" Black asked.

"Well, we know Trenton Hart figured out Poe's after death

plan, and it's why he wanted everyone wiped out." He tapped on his keyboard some more. "What happens if we're all gone? Where does the power go?"

If it was possible for a heart to stop and for the person to remain alive, that's what was happening to me. "I..."

"You never thought that far ahead because the possibilities were never there. In the event Black died, it goes to Quill. Same with Christopher and Snow. And if the Manos' die, then it gets transferred to Black. You loop everything to each other. But." He held up a finger. "And yes, I know it's insane, if you all die, where does it go?"

"Who'd take it to court?" Phin asked. "Trenton would get it back."

"Exactly," Lee said. "I'm sure whoever is working for him has been promised some huge percentage to make it all happen."

There was so much information being tossed around right now my brain needed to categorize it.

"Hold on," I said loud enough that everyone listened.

"Black, who took the agreement to hit Menagerie?"

"As far as I know it's open still. While the fifty million is a lot, Menagerie won't be easy to take down. Sometimes the price isn't worth it."

Phin laughed humorlessly. "But taking you down was okay?"

"Do I look like I've been taken down. Menagerie offered to take me out. Robin said when Trenton was giving hits she stepped up to go after me. He accepted, likely not caring who killed me, just that I was dead. And then she sat on it."

I suddenly knew how to keep Menagerie alive. "Fair enough, take the contract," I told Black.

His eyes widened and he chuckled. "Why would I do that?"

"You'll be doing for Menagerie what they did for you, keeping them safe," Phin answered.

"Don't you think the second they see I took it, they'll know what's up?"

It was Christopher who answered. "You have a target on your back, and I'll guess it reopened with Menagerie failing to complete their contract. Talos and Peluda are contracted to kill me and Poe, they aren't likely to take either contract right now. We got a lot of their people. In some ways, Trenton Hart putting out that contract was to see what others out there would help him."

"Can't you accept it anonymously?" Phin asked.

"Trenton had an open call. He likely asked Peluda or Talos to set up the hit, like you said Christopher, they're threadbare. If I accept, and give a false name no one has heard of, it'll look fake and the hit will be removed and reissued without me getting an invite."

"We'll watch the contract and see if it gets picked up. If it doesn't, we know they're safe. We can deal with it if it does," Lee said. "Did you give Menagerie a heads up?"

"Yeah, I gave them a heads up. We'll watch it and deal with it if it becomes a bigger issue."

With that settled for now, I brought up the next issue. "Now, what are the chances Trenton will be aiming to wipe us out on Friday?"

"But it would all go to Quill and Snow and I'm still alive," Phin said.

"We're working under the assumption they think you're not, Phin. And picking off Snow and Quill will be easier, no offense," I said to Christopher and Black.

"I'd say it's a huge possibility," Lee answered. "So, let's start from the beginning."

And all the arrangements for Friday now had to change. It was going to be a long night, so I let Sara know we'd have guests for dinner and to let Snow, who was currently hanging out with Adelaide and Simon, know. I wasn't getting a lot of time to hang with Addy, and I made a promise to make it up to her. She was enjoying spending time with Simon. She didn't get enough time around kids, and I knew she really needed that.

Riordan showed up when we all sat down to eat dinner. He was stuck doing some security thing and brought Lee information on his equipment and such that would help them on Friday. Going through Riordan's business would hopefully buy us time. Riordan had a few men that worked for him who he trusted the most. They were going to trail behind on Friday and stay out of sight. Because Trenton was likely going to be looking for Christopher and Black's men, they wouldn't notice them.

"The fact we gave Trenton only the day and time, but not the where yet, is probably the only reason a bomb won't be a possibility," Riordan said in between bites.

"Unless we get there before Trenton, in which case he could RPG the place." Snow wasn't helping with responses like that.

"Yeah, that can be easily explained away," I deadpanned, earning myself the finger from Snow.

"And a bomb can?" he countered.

"A bomb can be said to be a gas leak. Someone seeing a rocket head toward a location and then boom, can't," Lee said, and he was right. I was planning for it to be in a public place. I didn't want casualties from innocent bystanders.

"Okay, my guys watch the place the night before. You decide where and they'll case it," Riordan said. "My guess is they'll use snipers or it'll be an internal hit that'll be delayed with how little time he'll have to prepare."

"Sounds like our best option," Black agreed, and we spent the rest of dinner listening to everyone talking about video games and how Teddy was unnaturally talented.

Chapter Thirty

Phin

The days leading up to Friday were eventful in the way one might think we were going to a royal affair. Poe was fitted for an outfit that looked like something he'd normally wear, but it was flame resistant, bullet proof, and had tiny cameras all over it. Christopher and Black were put into suits befitting their style, but with the same protections. Lee had them designed, and they were impressive.

Snow stopped by with Lee to test the equipment, so we'd be able to hear and see everything. Teddy had been spending a lot of time with Adelaide, and she told me he was her teddy bear because he snuggled, then laughed when she realized how perfect his name was for him.

Elliott came by every day and helped with my strength training. I was getting better every day. Black told me there was a pool in the building on the floor the gym was on. For two nights, Poe and I went there and swam together.

When Friday morning came, so did the storms. It was a horrific thunderstorm that woke me, and the rain came down in sheets. While a rainy day was a blah day, it was perfect against the enemy. Outside visibility would be bad for snipers, but that also meant bad for their own. Everyone agreed it would be an internal hit.

Because Black didn't want Snow, Quill, and anyone else that would gain something from their death separated, everyone came to the penthouse. Riordan, Ginger, Donny, and Mace were staying with us at the penthouse. With Poe would be Black, Christopher,

Jones, Frank, and five of Riordan's guys nearby, and three other men Christopher had with him.

Simon and Joey were also at our penthouse keeping Adelaide occupied. Teddy said he'd be with the kids since he had to watch Rosie.

Quill, Snow, and I would all huddle around the screen with our headphones and listen as our men hopefully made this mess go away. I wasn't optimistic, but I grabbed at every ounce of hope I could.

"When are you giving Trenton the meeting place?" Quill asked Poe.

"I told him to leave his place at two, and I would send the location when he's en route."

"Oh, bet he just *loved* that." My uncle hated relinquishing control. Just seeing how he was trying to get it back with what Poe did proved that.

"I don't give a fuck what he likes." Poe was livid, but aside from swearing, you wouldn't know. He looked pristine, placid, and perfect. His mask was in place, and he was ready to stare down the devil himself.

"My men are at the location now," Christopher said as he entered the living room.

"Excellent, and your men, Riordan?" Poe asked.

"Two are in a painter's van across the way. I spoke with the owner of that building, and they agreed to help me out and let them pretend they were assessing the building for a painting job. My other three are a block away listening in."

"Okay, gentlemen, let's get going." Poe came over to me and held my face in his hands. "I love you."

"Don't do that." He raised his brows when I snapped at him. "This I love you and goodbye shit."

He released a breath. He hadn't put his glasses on yet, so I was able to look into the deep dark pools of his eyes.

"I don't know how this will turn out, Phin. We've done everything to have the upper hand here but I just… I don't know. So, if I want to tell you I love you, you should just shut up and let me."

"Don't die."

He chuckled. "I promise my goal is to live."

He pressed his lips to mine, and a second later, I opened for him. I kissed him like it was goodbye. I kissed life into him, hope, prayer, anything to make him come back to me. When he pulled away, the loss made my heart ache.

"I'll see you soon." He winked and began walking toward the doors. I looked around the room and saw Christopher, Black, Bill, and Jones all doing the same thing with their partners. Sometimes doing what had to be done was a dangerous gamble. I just wanted us all to make it through this.

Adelaide gave Poe a big hug, Simon did the same for Christopher, and Joey for Black and Jones. After they left, a silence descended over the room. Fans from Lee's equipment were all you could hear. It would take a few minutes for them to get to the garage and into the cars, so we were allowed a moment to let the enormity of the situation sink in.

"Okay, then." Lee broke the scared shitless silence and like a switch was hit, we all moved.

"Sara, would you please get something for the kids to eat and maybe set them up in the TV room? They can do whatever: video games, movies, anything."

"Sure thing." She left and made sure Adelaide and the others followed her.

After she was gone, Snow, Quill, Riordan, Ginger, and I sat around Lee. Teddy was off setting Rosie up for a nap, but I didn't imagine he'd come sit with us. He was all lover, no fighter. Mace was walking around the penthouse with Donny staying vigilant.

"Cameras are working great," Ginger said as we all watched

our guys getting into cars. Poe, Christopher, and Black were in separate vehicles. We wanted to keep them apart just in case.

"How's the sound?" I tapped my earpiece, not hearing anything.

"One moment." Lee hit a few keys. "How about now?"

I heard Poe talking to the driver about where they were going. I knew they'd arrive before he even let Trenton know the location. Black was going in first. Then Christopher, and finally Poe. There was no way Trenton would do anything until they were all together. I was happy to see that Bill drove with Poe, as well. Each man had one person with them. Frank was with Christopher; Black had a woman named Jaclyn with him. She was another assassin, and Lee explained she was as loyal as they came.

No one was talking much, but I listened all the same. The cameras were crisp, and I loved how they went all around their suits. If someone was coming up behind them, Lee could notify them.

Quill had arranged to have Quirks and Perks, a café/bookstore his friend Mel officially owned now, be closed for this. It would be tricky keeping people out, but the guys in the painter's truck said they'd try to thwart people from entering saying it was closed for repairs. Mel told Quill she'd be working behind the counter because people knew the place. If she wasn't there, it would be suspicious. We had to let her in on some information, and she said the second it got ugly she'd go hide or run out the back.

Quill was not a happy man knowing his best friend was in danger, but Mel was stubborn and refused to budge.

"They're pulling up to the café now," Quill said.

"Showtime." Lee hit record and we sat back and watched.

Chapter Thirty-One

Poe

To the unassuming, Quirks and Perks appeared to be open for business. There was a man sitting at one of the small round tables with a cup of coffee and an open laptop. I knew that was one of Christopher's men. The other two sat together and appeared to be having some sort of business meeting. Also, Christopher's men. Across the way I saw the painters and knew they had a camera pointed at us and were watching our backs.

Quill's friend, Mel, was standing behind the counter cleaning one of the coffee pots. She promised she had the back door securely latched. If they came in that way, it wouldn't be quiet.

Christopher and Black had gone in before me, and they'd put together a few tables. There was no point hiding they were together. I went up to the counter to order a coffee.

"Hello," Mel said with a slightly frightened smile.

"Good afternoon. May I have a French vanilla coffee, medium?"

I'd texted Trenton ten minutes before letting him know where we'd be meeting, so I expected him soon.

I paid and went to fix my coffee. I'd just sat down with Christopher and Black when the door opened, and in strode two men I didn't recognize, and one I most certainly did.

"Ah, Trent, there you are," I said, feeling great joy at the tick in his cheek. He was an older man in his late sixties almost seventy. His hair was streaked with white and silver, he had a gut, but it wasn't insane, it was what I called an aged body. He stood at six foot two, clean shaven, fair skin, and wore a ridiculously expensive gray suit. He was as monochrome as my eyesight. He wasn't ugly, he was average.

"Poe." His voice was deep and gravelly and dripped with disdain as he said my name.

"And who are you two gentlemen?" I asked, looking at the two who stood like pillars beside Trenton.

"Peluda and Talos," Black said as he stood. Neither of the men made a move as Black strode over. "What interesting company you two are keeping these days." He was about a foot from them when he gestured toward me and Christopher. "As you can see, you failed."

"It won't happen again," one of the men, I assumed was Peluda since he wore the same medallion Lee showed me belonged to his men, replied. He was rail thin, tall, had long black hair. I couldn't tell through the gray coloring what shade his clothes were, but they were expensive. His nose had a hook to it, and his eyes were almost too small for his face.

"We weren't given proper information," Talos said as he side eyed Trenton. He was a gorgeous black man. Even I could see that. But knowing he was the one who came into my home and tried to kill my family left me with an awful taste in my mouth. Unlike Peluda, Talos wore a more casual outfit; jeans, and some color shirt. He seemed unbothered by today's events.

"Let me ask you something, Talos. Had you known what you were up against, had you been given all the information, would you have still proceeded with this hit?" Black inched closer to Talos, again no one moved.

"Don't answer that," Trenton interrupted. "Let's get on with this meeting."

Black's murderous glare stared Trenton down. I thought Black was going to tear Trenton's face off, but with a small sneer, he went back to his seat, and we waited for them to get drinks.

Trenton then sat with his back to the door while Talos and Peluda stood behind him. He was just as untrusting as we were.

"We have a serious problem," I started, only to have Trenton raise a single brow in response. "You're trying to kill us, and your two idiot assassins just admitted it."

It was true, Trenton had played dumb on the phone, but Talos and Peluda came right out and said they tried and failed. That did change things slightly.

"What these two do on their own time is…" Trenton acted nonchalant about it, but I wasn't having it. He'd see why the power I held was feared.

Slamming my fists on the table got everyone's attention. "Don't play dumb with me, Trent. I have no time for these games. You tried to kill me, and Christopher Manos, and it seems Menagerie is the only smart one and didn't see the contract to completion. You've made enemies, Trent, that even if I wanted to protect you from, I can't."

"Please, you'd be happy if I keeled over dead." He leaned forward, hands together resting on the table. "Your claim to the Hart name is bullshit. Your power is bullshit. You tied things up as tight as possible, and with no choice given, I had to get it back this way."

"You chose violence?" I was gritting my teeth; anger was trying to get the better of me.

"I chose the only way. You give us an allowance. It's our fucking money, Poe, not yours!" his voice boomed in the café.

"I'm going to step in here," Christopher said in a low timber. "Whether or not you like how Poe handled anything doesn't change the fact you tried to kill me and my family." He smiled just then, and it was so shark-like and sinister I would've slinked back if it was aimed my way.

"If you've been doing your homework, Trenton, you'll know I don't give people second chances when it comes to my family.

You're not the first person who tried to hurt what's mine, and I'm sure you won't be the last. But, every single person who's attempted is now dead. I'm sure you're aware." He leaned back and let those words sink in.

Trenton's expression was unreadable, there was slight fear, but he was also invested in the war at this point. I wasn't sure what he'd do.

"What's the point to this meeting if you just promised you'd kill me regardless of anything?" Trenton chuckled. "Counterproductive if you ask me. How do you remain so successful, Chrissy?"

The Chrissy remark was strictly to get Christopher to react. But he didn't, Bill did. He'd been there the whole time in the booth behind us. He walked right up to the table, paying no mind to the two assassins getting ready to block whatever he was going to do.

"Call him Chrissy one more time, and I'll kill you with a fucking straw, motherfucker!" He pointed at Trenton.

"Call your rabid dog off, Christopher. He'll get himself killed." He turned and looked up to where Talos and Peluda stood behind him. "If he comes near me again, kill him."

Had Trenton gone mad?

"Let me ask you something, Trent," I said, happy when Bill stepped back, but he didn't go to the booth. He stood behind Christopher where Frank was, as well.

"What?"

"How are you going to pay these men?" I gestured to the assassins. "I've frozen all your accounts, assets, everything. I doubt they are doing this out of the goodness of their cold dead hearts."

There are moments in our lives when we feel like we are untouchable. At the highest point of perfection. We feel safe, and ahead of the game. It's amazing. I was in that moment thinking

Talos and Peluda would question him. But when neither man flinched, and Trenton smiled, it was like someone pushed me off that peak of invulnerability. His next words had the ground coming up to meet me and crushing me whole.

"Let me ask you a question, Poe. What makes you think Phineas and the others are safe in Black's ivory tower right now?"

Chapter Thirty-Two

Phin

Being away from them and watching this all play out was beyond frustrating. The back and forth banter was angering me. Snow patted my hand a few times when I lightly pounded the table. How was Trenton so confident and carefree? When Christopher basically told him he was going to die no matter how this played out, I would have thought he'd flinch even a little bit, but nothing.

Every so often, between walking the penthouse, Mace came over to see what was happening. He didn't say anything until he heard Bill shouting at Trenton.

"Hot head," he muttered, and then went back to walking the floors, not worried at all that Bill would get himself killed. He clearly had a lot of faith in his man.

It all felt off. Nothing seemed like it was going how we thought it would. I watched the screen where the painters had a camera set to the café, there was no activity outside the place. I then noticed Riordan's men were reporting nothing.

"Something's wrong," I said, and everyone in the room turned to me.

"Why do you say that?" Donny asked.

"If I said it was my gut feeling, would that be enough?"

Mace and Riordan had some sort of silent conversation and then nodded. "Our guts are all we have sometimes," Riordan said and pointed to Donny. "Check the building."

"Wait, here?" I asked. "I meant there." Gesturing to the screen, I saw a back and forth with Poe and Trenton. Poe seemed relaxed.

"No, you're right," Snow said. "It's not right."

Just then we heard Trenton's words.

"Let me ask you a question, Poe, what makes you think Phineas and the others are safe in Black's ivory tower right now?"

"Red alert," Lee said into everyone's earpieces. Teddy, Tony, everyone had them in case of an emergency.

I had just stood when the building shook. "What the hell was that?"

Teddy came running in, Rosie on his hip, Simon, Joey, and Adelaide on his tail. "What's happening?"

Just then we heard a loud explosion and the building shook again. Alarms sounded and the lights went out.

"Roof!" Donny yelled. "Get to the fucking roof now!" He raced back into the room. "They're hitting the building, fucking move." He grabbed Snow's hand and ran. We dropped everything.

"Tony, get Addy!" He didn't hesitate to scoop her up. Everyone was racing toward the doors, except Lee. "Let's go." I grabbed his arm.

"I can't. I have to transfer this to my travel laptop. The power surge wiped it, I need to redo it."

"Fuck that," Ginger yelled as he pulled on Lee's other arm.

"Ginger, if I don't, I can't help them defend themselves. All the defense is in here. I have to transfer it." The building shook again, and the sound of a helicopter above us made me realize we were being lifted out of here.

"Lee, please," Ginger was crying. "I stay if you stay."

"No." He turned to me. "Phin needs your help to get out of here. He isn't strong enough."

"Then I stay, too."

Lee's eyes narrowed. And his gaze went from me to Ginger. "Fuck," he shouted and dropped everything. He didn't hesitate to lift me, and I was shocked by his strength.

"Is the building clear?" Ginger was speaking into the microphone as we raced up the stairs to the roof.

"All clear," a voice said in my ear.

"Where the fuck are you?" I heard Mace yelling.

"Coming," I answered, just as we burst through the roof door.

Lights and pillows were still up there from my date with Poe, and I ached to be back there in that moment.

"We have to climb up to the helipad," Ginger said, pointing to the raised area.

That was going to be very hard for me, but I'd do it. "You two go first, it'll take me longer." The building shook again, and I felt a drop like it was about to fall.

"Ginger first. Get to the top, then Phin, I'll bring in the rear, we can get you up there."

As we climbed up the ladder, I could hear who I thought was Jones screaming into his headset for us, but the equipment must have been malfunctioning because whenever anyone tried to respond they weren't hearing us.

"Gimme your hand." Ginger was reaching down to me and I stretched. He gripped and pulled while Lee pushed me up.

"Come on!" Riordan was shouting by the helicopter. The next explosion was so powerful it felt like the ground fell and I crashed to the cement.

"Hurry!" someone screamed, and I realized it was Addy. I looked up from the ground and saw her blue eyes from the helicopter door. "Daddy!" she shrilled. With everything in me, I stood.

Lee and Ginger each took one of my arms and we raced to the helicopter. I was practically thrown inside but I didn't complain. Riordan hopped in and slid the door shut. "Go."

We lifted off just as the roof began to collapse. Adelaide was sobbing and clung to me. I kissed her hair and tried to calm her down. I didn't know if Poe was okay or anyone else. *How'd this go sideways so fast?*

There was a cacophony of voices all trying to get information on Poe and the others but the equipment wasn't working.

The farther we got from the building, the better we were able to see it. It was like certain floors were hit, each damaging the integrity of the structure. We were far enough away when it could stand no more and collapsed to the ground. I closed my eyes, and silently prayed the building was in fact cleared out.

"Shit," I heard Quill say. His eyes were glistening. "That's Black's life."

"No," I said as I took Quill's hand. "You're Black's life."

"Where are we going?" Simon shouted over the loudness of the helicopter.

"Where can we go?" Snow spoke as he kept trying to fiddle with his phone, likely hoping he'd get Christopher.

We couldn't leave Haven Hart; we couldn't go anywhere near where Poe and the others were. It had to be a place either Trenton wouldn't find us or he wouldn't think we'd dare go, therefore he'd be unprepared.

I listened as everyone was listing off places and ideas. Each worse than the other. Every property mentioned belonged to either Black or Christopher. It was no good. Our house was destroyed, and we weren't going back there until it was rebuilt and this mess was over.

Think, Phin, think. And then it hit me…

"This place has more hiding spots than anywhere I've ever been," Poe said as he laughed and followed me through the maze of halls.

"Wanna see something cool?" I asked him as I opened a door

leading outside. It was the summer of my fourteenth year, and Poe had the weird idea to explore every nook and cranny of the Hart castle.

"I'd be upset if I didn't," he joked, and I opened the door. "Whoa!"

"Yeah, if you take this tunnel, it'll lead you all the way to the city."

"That's crazy! Where else?" He walked through and the lights kicked on.

"Every mile, there's a new door that takes you to a different place. My great great grandfather built it. He was always so paranoid, saying how the Hart family was a target because of the power they wielded. He wanted ways to run if he needed it. My grams told me about it."

We walked for a while and came to one door. "Is it locked?" Poe put his hand on the doorknob.

"Nah, see if it opens."

It was rough, but together, we managed to push the door open. A sign hung in our view. "Fifth Avenue," Poe whispered. "Holy shit, Phin. These tunnels take us through the whole city?"

I shook my head. "No, there's others in the suburban area. They used them for prohibition. My grams said when those were built her father made sure they didn't interfere with these."

"You can get out of the Hart estate and go anywhere with these." He laughed excitedly.

"Or get in."

"I know where to go!" I yelled, glad when everyone heard me.

"Where?" Riordan squeezed his way over to me.

"Find the nearest remote field that's not too far from the city."

"I'm not leaving us open," Riordan scoffed.

"No, I promise, it'll be for a minute maybe five max."

"There's a field where that warehouse used to be on Tenth Avenue. Would that work?" Quill said.

"Tenth, yeah, the distribution center is there, right?" Quill nodded. "Great, get us there."

"And then what?" Mace asked.

"Then I get you into the Hart estate."

Snow's eyes widened. "That's suicide."

"It's perfect," Lee said. "How will that work?"

"You'll have to trust me."

No one said anymore after that. Riordan gave the pilot the information, and we rushed off to the location. I only hoped Poe and the others were okay, and we could get a message out to them.

Chapter Thirty-Three

Poe

Trenton was laughing now. Once the words left his mouth about the safety of our loved ones, Jones and Bill immediately stepped away, likely to check if everyone was all right.

"There's not a chance any of your people, or theirs, could get into my building." Black gestured to Peluda and Talos.

"You're right, because we're here, aren't we?" Trenton held out his hands almost like he was saying ta-da.

Christopher got up and walked over to Bill who was talking to someone. I couldn't hear what he was saying or what Christopher was saying, but I was getting tired of this. Trenton wasn't going to stop. He mentioned Phin, but he could've just meant him being in a vegetative state. I couldn't go near that. I wanted to see who else in the Hart family was involved so we knew what we were dealing with. I opened my mouth to say something when the ground rumbled slightly.

"Was that an earthquake?" Mel asked from by the counter.

Trenton chuckled and something in his glare told me he knew exactly what that was.

"Lee, come in," I heard Jones say. "Ginger?"

"What's going on?" Black was thunderous. He stood and rounded on Trenton just as another rumble shook the ground. Glasses fell from the shelves, shattering as they hit the floor. Trenton laughed louder, and when Black charged, he was met with two lethal looking guns pointed at his face. Talos held one, Peluda the other.

This caused a domino effect. The five men who had been sitting in the café stood and pulled out their own weapons.

"Seems we have a bit of a standoff, Trenton," Christopher said as he walked away from Bill.

"Do we?" He looked around, he hadn't even stood up through all of this. "How I see it is all I have to do now is kill all of you and everything will be reverted back to the true Hart bloodline." He narrowed his eyes at me.

"What do you mean all you have to do is kill us?" Black's voice was low, threatening, and rumbled like the earth was right now.

"It's no earthquake," Trenton said, and he finally did stand up. "That's your tower crumbling to ash, and all you love dying with it."

No! I whirled around and raced over to the window. From here you could see the top of Black's building. I had to know. All I saw was a helicopter hovering above. There was so much smoke and dust.

"Black."

A moment later, the sound became louder, the ground shook, and glass shattered. Someone slammed me to the floor, and it felt like the world was ending. It was infinite carnage and breathing became impossible as dust clogged my throat and I started hacking.

"Don't move," someone said in my ear. It sounded familiar, but I couldn't place it in that moment—I was trying to figure out what was happening.

When nothing was shaking anymore, I fought whoever was on top of me. They let me up, and I stood only to realize it was Black who had shielded me.

"You risked your life for me."

He shrugged. "It's what I do."

"Is everyone okay?" Bill came over to us, he was covered in debris, and he had tiny cuts over one side of his face, most likely from the glass.

"I am, Black seems to be." I searched the café. It was dirty and there was glass everywhere, but it seemed fairly intact. Mel jumped up from behind the counter.

"Out back. The dipshit who kept laughing ran out back."

Bill and Black raced out the door while I helped Frank and Christopher up. I called over to Jones who grunted. "Any word on the others?"

"I can't get through. I kept trying. Lee was speaking, but it broke up then it was dead air."

Black and Bill rushed back in empty handed. "They're gone."

"Did they think the explosion or whatever that was, was going to kill us?" one of Christopher's men said.

"I think they think it's just us left." Black tried his cell phone, only to realize it was cracked and not working. "We need to get to the building."

"It's gone." There was no hiding the vacancy in my tone. "Just before all this—" I waved my hand at the mess "—I saw a helicopter hovering over the roof, there was smoke it was…" I couldn't think of it.

"Was the chopper rescuing them?" Bill asked.

A surge of anger pushed through me. "What about my eyes makes you think I have super vision?"

"Oh, excuse me if I—" Bill started but Christopher stood between us.

"Not the time. Everyone we love is in there. We need to find them. Let's move. Frank?"

"I'll get a car."

He walked out and I saw him run across the way to where Black's men were. They were covered in earth. It was then I saw people milling around the street crying, screaming, utterly terrified.

"What's his plan, to rule Haven Hart with fire and fear?" I whispered to no one, but Christopher answered.

"He wouldn't be the first to try."

"Boss." Frank came back in. "I've got a car coming. Riordan's men, they're here, too. One of them got a hold of Riordan, he was in a helicopter."

That had to be good news. "Did everyone get out?"

"I'm sorry, I don't know. But I have a meeting location. We need to get there now."

Ignoring the ache in my head from being slammed to the ground and the twinge in my ankle, I followed Frank and the others out the door. Riordan's men were there and a few of us piled in, myself being one of them. The rest got in the SUV behind us.

"Where are we going?" Donny asked.

"The distribution center on Tenth," one of Riordan's guys said.

I had no idea why we'd be going there, but what I did know was that no place seemed safe. We drove down Fifth and past the Out Of Focus Gallery. The glass was blown out, but other than that, there didn't appear to be any other damage. Fire trucks, police cars, and ambulances were filling the streets fast. The driver maneuvered around wandering people and frantic drivers.

I closed my eyes and thought of Adelaide and Phin. I hoped they were alive and safe. Oh God, I didn't know what I'd do if they weren't.

"There's Riordan," Donny said as we drove around the back of the distribution center.

Once the van stopped, Donny got out and Riordan ran over to us. "Thank God you're all safe."

"What happened?" Donny asked at the same time I asked if everyone was alive and okay.

"Everyone's in the distribution center, follow me." *He said everyone.*

We stepped inside and there they were. Phin was sitting on a small crate, Adelaide on his lap hugging him fiercely. When his gaze met mine, I finally breathed.

"Phin, Addy." I rushed over to them the same time I saw everyone else reaching for their loved ones. Nothing mattered right then. We all survived. I didn't know how, and I didn't know if Trenton knew that. But as I embraced Addy and Phin, I chose not to think about that just then. All I wanted in that moment was to feel. They lived, I lived.

Chapter Thirty-Four

Phin

It was a flurry of hugs, tears, and questions for a while. Finally, the woman Black was with, Jaclyn I believed, whistled loudly.

"Okay, let's chill. First, I was outside Quirks and Perks the whole time during the meeting, walking the perimeter. There was nothing until the building exploded. No snipers, nothing. I was talking with Mace and Ginger throughout and it was quiet, and then it all happened at once. It seems it was localized to the building. No RPGs; nothing."

"Which means the bombs were planted inside your building?" I asked Black who seemed almost shell-shocked.

"How would that be possible?"

"I've been rolling it around in my head since it happened. The building is secure, nothing could get in like that. It would be detected," Lee said as Ginger wrapped his arms around him.

"There's an explanation, there always is." Ginger kissed his cheek, but Lee was clearly beating himself up over this.

"I know you, there's no way you had everything in that building. You have backups off site. I'm sure there's cameras, we can look at them and figure it out." Jones had Lee's face in his hands. "This isn't on you."

"He was trying to transfer everything over when we were leaving, but we had to go. The systems were malfunctioning, so I'm not sure how much would have gone through." I knew Lee was going to be upset by that, and knowing it may have information we needed had to be killing him.

"Hold on." Teddy stepped forward. His curly hair was like a

ball of frizz from everything that happened, he had a smudge of dirt across his nose, and Rosie in his arms. She was a mess and her eyes were puffy from crying, but she wasn't hurt. "Nothing that happened today in that building is going to matter."

"I beg to disagree," Black said.

Teddy rolled his eyes and waved the big man off. "You think whoever did this planted those bombs there today?"

"So, we go back in the footage." Snow looked over at Lee. "Can we do that?"

"Yeah, but I'd need to get to it. I have it in one of the safe houses. That's if the safehouse is still standing."

"Okay, we need to get you over there," Poe said.

"Wait." Carefully I stood. "Yes, we need to investigate how and where it went wrong, but we know the who and we know the why. Trenton Hart did this and he did it to kill us. The fact we all crammed ourselves in there was perfect for him. Honestly, I'm surprised he didn't blow the building when we were all in there." I said to Lee, "I get you want to figure out the flaw, but that's not important. Getting to the upper ground is."

"And where is that exactly?" Quill asked. "Why are we in a distribution center?"

I faced Poe with a smile. "Remember the tour I gave you one summer? When I asked you if you wanted to see something cool?"

His brow crinkled in confusion for the briefest moment, then realization dawned on him.

"The tunnels."

"What tunnels?" Christopher asked.

I spent the next few minutes explaining to them about my great great grandfather, the tunnels, and the likelihood my uncle didn't know about them.

"Sort of like the tunnels under a few of my safehouses," Black said to Riordan. "That's how we were able to trick Emma into thinking you died. They move throughout the city. Are you talking about those?"

"Similar but different passageways," I answered.

"They must not have been on the blueprints." Lee walked over to me.

"They wouldn't be. They were never documented and because my grandmother only ever told me, and I only ever told Poe, we're the only two living who were aware of them."

"I forgot about them."

"So, you never added them in the blueprints." Lee seemed appeased.

"It's a good thing, too, because your uncle would likely have used those." Mace was helping Adelaide with a very upset Countess Cocoa Puff. They made one of the tiny crates into a holding spot for her and she was meowing.

"As cool as this is, how does that help us? We can get beneath the city and what, live like moles?" Frank huffed.

"No. We can take the tunnels to the Hart estate."

"I was wondering when you said that earlier how you intended on getting us there unseen." Seeing Lee smile was a relief. I knew he'd continue to beat himself up, but he needed to be in the moment.

"We'll be going right into enemy territory, why would we do that?" Black looked at me like I was nuts.

"They'd never expect that, and from what I gathered, my uncle hasn't lived there in some time. We'd be able to get in undetected. See what Harts there are living on the property and go from there. It's not a perfect plan, but it's the best we have right now."

They all seemed to be thinking about it, so I sat back down next to Addy who was petting her kitty.

"It's a good plan, Daddy." She smiled at me.

"You okay, baby?"

She shrugged. "I wanna go home. I don't know why people want to hurt us. But I know you and Papa will figure it out."

She had so much confidence in me and I didn't want to disappoint her.

"We can't go in without protection. And is it wise to bring the kids with us?" Donny said.

"Problem is we don't know what or where is safe. What we do know is they're better off with us," Poe answered. "They'll bring in the back, guarded." He faced me, worry marred his features. "I can't be sure your uncle knows you're moving, but I don't think it matters at this point. Are you okay with this, will you be able to move in those tunnels?"

"I'll be fine, but Donny is right, we need protection."

"I can help there." Riordan stepped forward. "My business wasn't hit. There're guns there."

"Your business was built from the ground up. It's not directly connected to where the tunnels intersect." Poe knew this better than I did since Riordan's company was fairly new, and I had to play catch up on all the new things that had happened in the three years I was asleep.

"What do you suggest?" Ginger asked.

"You know where my business is, Poe. How close will the tunnels get us to there?"

"Hallman's Hardware. It's a half mile from your place."

"That's no good, no one can be seen carrying a small arsenal even a block right now, not with everything going on in the city." Riordan scratched the back of his head and paced.

"They'll have to drive there, no choice." Christopher turned to Black. "We have the van and SUV. A group has to go and they'll meet us back here. We'll have to strategize before we walk into the Hart estate anyway." He assessed the area. "Who owns this center?"

Poe chuckled. "I'll have it closed for tomorrow. With the

building collapse, the excuse is warranted." That explained who owned it, then. So much had changed, and yet nothing at all.

Christopher gave a curt nod. "We need to figure out who's going to get the weapons. It'll take time, most streets will be closed off. The rest of us will have to get comfortable. Best we can do is not act rashly. Let things settle outside for the day and night. Tomorrow we move."

"I'll go," Jaclyn stood.

"Okay, you two." Christopher pointed to two of his men. "You go with her."

"And you two. You know where everything is," Riordan said to his guys. "Five-person team. Gather anything and everything you can for this. We won't move out until you return."

"Let's move." Jaclyn started jogging toward the exit.

"Guess we know who's in charge," one of Christopher's men said with a chuckle. But no one challenged Jaclyn, and soon they were out and moving to get protection.

Chapter Thirty-Five

Poe

There were three large distribution centers in Haven Hart. The one we were all currently in stored products for several large companies. One was a major auto parts company which didn't help us at all. However, the other companies that used this center were extremely helpful for us. Sleep, Eat, Live was a major online company that sold everything. We searched all the areas and were able to put some mattresses together, grab a few pillows, find clothes for everyone to change into. There was even bath supplies. We used the employee bathrooms to clean up as best we could, and when I came out, Ginger was laughing.

"What's so funny?"

"Their breakroom. There were a bunch of frozen pizzas and sodas. The explosion didn't wipe out the electrical here, miraculously, so I'm heating them up. Food, beds, we're doing well. When I was on the streets, I would've given my left nut to be locked in a distribution center."

"I hear that," Snow agreed. "We'll be fine for the evening. Bill found paper and pens over there, so let's sit and figure out what we're going to do when we seize the castle."

I stopped by the office on my way to the floor of mattresses we'd created and called the center's manager. When I explained the place was shut down tomorrow due to the chaos, he sounded relieved. I was sure nobody wanted to come anywhere near Haven Hart right now, and if they were stuck in it, they were locking themselves inside. He told me he'd let drivers and such know, and I said goodbye and joined the others who were already deep in talks about the next day.

The sirens in the background got quieter as the night pressed on. It was close to midnight by the time we figured out a plan. Jaclyn and the others returned shortly after, and a bunch of the guys went over to inspect what they had. I had many hours clocked with target practice, but it wasn't my forte. I would do what I had to, I'd just rather not. Tony and Jones seemed to be getting along. My other security hung back and listened. The loss of Missy and Logan hit them hard, and I knew they wanted their revenge just like the rest of us.

"Is this memory foam?" Teddy asked as he tried to bounce on one of the mattresses. "It's like it hugs me. It's perfect, I love it."

"What do you sleep on at home?" Quill asked from his mattress. Black was currently dealing with the weapons with Christopher, Riordan, and the others.

"Riordan and I have a sleep number bed." He shrugged. "It's okay, but it's a king size and I don't like when I have my side up and his is down. I can't cuddle. I've been thinking of secretly replacing it."

We all chuckled at Teddy's plan. Snow, Teddy, Quill, and I together again, like we were when we meditated. I used to want Phin with me and now he was.

"I just realized our meditation circle is back," I said. Snow turned to me, his eyes sad, yet he wore a small smile.

"I did say I'd have to do something drastic to get you back, didn't I?" he joked, and we all shared in a moment of levity.

Teddy put his hand out in the middle of the circle. "Promise, here and now, when this mess is over, there's no more secrets. No lies. We won't slip away from each other again, and we'll be friends until the end of the world."

Quill was the first to put his hand in. "I promise to be even more awesome than I am now and be here when any of you need me."

Snow was next. "I love you guys, and while I'd love to say

our lives will be smooth sailing after this, that's probably not true, but we'll do it all together."

Phin looked at me, a huge smile on his face as he too put his hand on the pile. "I'm sorry for this mess and that it caused a rift between all of you. I hope you'll welcome me into this meditation madness circle, and I too promise to be here for any of you whenever."

The three other men nodded, and then all eyes were on me. I stared at the pile of hands, all stacked in various shades of gray. My friends, who was I kidding? My family.

I placed my hand on the top. "You have my word, I will always answer when you call. I'll be there for as long as this world allows me to be. Thank you for your friendship, your loyalty, and for never giving up on me."

"Can we hug?" Teddy asked softly, and we burst out laughing. But hug, we did. Like a pile of exhausted puppies, we wrapped our arms around each other in a snug embrace and laughed.

It was close to two by the time everyone tucked in. Because of the events of the day and everyone being tired, two-man teams got one-hour shifts. As I held Phin close to me, I silently prayed this would end well for our side. I hoped when we entered the Hart estate the next day, we'd find none of the residents there had any idea what Trenton was up to. More than anything, I hoped we'd find Trenton and make this nightmare end.

The next morning, I woke to the fresh smell of coffee and for the briefest moment, before I opened my eyes, I thought I'd dreamed it all. But I hadn't. Tony was sitting on the mattress beside me waving the aroma in my face to wake me.

"Ginger and Lee went and got coffee and bagels for everyone.

With what happened yesterday, cops are everywhere. Trenton won't be doing anything."

I sat up and gratefully took the coffee. It tasted like hope. Well, maybe not, but I was exhausted and I needed whatever I could get my hands on.

"I was able to use the computer in the office. The news is all over this, and there's many people asking what the mayor and Hart family will be doing about all this." Lee sat on one of the crates, bagel in hand.

"Has the mayor held a press conference?" Phin's voice was sleepy, and I asked Tony if he could grab some coffee for him.

"No. My guess is he's waiting on you." Lee pointed to me and I realized I couldn't hide. I'd been too active in all things Haven Hart; to disappear now would be horrible. I had to rebuild what Trenton tore down.

"I'll call him after my coffee, and we'll have to figure out what to say. The mayor's office won't want to stay quiet much longer. It's a horrific message to send the people."

After I was more awake, I went into the manager's office and called the mayor. I told him I was rather busy with everything going on, and that he could quote the Hart family in saying the city had our support, and we'd be sure to help rebuild it to its former glory once the dust settled. He seemed pleased, and it bought me some time to hunt Trenton down and make all these years of surviving worth it.

Chapter Thirty-Six

Phin

As we all changed into comfortable clothes, Poe made a list. We'd have to reimburse everything we'd used, and even in the face of impending doom, my amazing husband was trying to keep things right with the city.

"Do we walk to the tunnel entrance or are we driving?" Angel, one of Tony's men, asked.

"There's an entrance close to here. We may be safer to walk just in case." I zipped up the light coat and rejected the handgun offered. "No, I don't have the coordination for that, but if you have a knife I'll take that." Angel handed me a wicked looking hunting knife and a sheath. I clipped it to my belt.

"Are you sure you'll be able to walk it?" Poe asked, and from anyone else I'd probably feel insulted, but his inquiry was genuine concern. In those tunnels, no one could be carried, there just wasn't room.

"I'll take it slow, promise."

"What about Countess Cocoa Puff?" Addy hugged her furball and that did present an issue. I was at a loss and not sure what to say when Lee spoke up.

"We need someone to drive to the Hart estate, as well. Someone situated close to the front gates but out of sight." He moved toward Adelaide. "How about the Countess goes in the van with the men headed over there. We can grab some food and water."

"Lou, Div, you two drive in one of the vans." Riordan was instructing his men, who agreed.

"Promise to take care of her?" Adelaide questioned the large blond man who was easily six foot five.

"Yes, milady." He smiled softly as he took the cat so tenderly in his hands.

"If we get in, someone will open the gates. Once inside, there are ways to secure it." Poe was securing a few weapons around his body per Black's request. He didn't want to, but when it was explained how unpredictable things had been and how we needed to be prepared for anything, Poe decided to concede.

"Sounds good. Why don't we go now? If we see anything from our line of sight, I'll let you know," the blond man said.

"Here." Lee handed him a cell phone. "We only have three. Service is spotty, but that's how you contact us."

He nodded and left with the other guy and Countess Cocoa Puff.

Half an hour later, we were well on our way, and I saw the first area where the tunnel was.

"How has no one seen this?" Quill asked as Black and Riordan chopped away overgrown brush that covered the entrance.

"No one was looking," Poe answered. "One thing I've discovered these past few years is this town sees what it wants, feels what it has to, and believes what it's told. If someone saw this and another said it was sealed for safety, then they'd walk away."

"Really?" Quill's brow arched. "If I'm told don't do something, I totally do it."

Poe smirked at his sassy friend. "Well, you're one of the rare birds in this town, trust me on that."

It took a lot of muscle, but we were able to turn the handle and open the tunnel entrance. The second Tony stepped in, the darkened place illuminated.

"Clearly it's maintained," Riordan said as he followed Tony.

"No one knows about these tunnels but me and Poe, well,

now you guys." I did wonder how the lights were working, but as we got farther in, we began to see they all did not in fact work. There were long spaces where they were off completely or flickering. We had two cell phones with flashlights and used those.

"Make a left at the next tunnel. We'll be walking for a while, but this will take us to the estate," I said.

Adelaide, Sara, and Patricia were in the center of the line, protected on all sides. Joey and Simon with them. They were all carrying water for us, and it was a good thing because halfway down the tunnel we had to break. While my stamina wasn't the best, some of these men were large and there were parts of the tunnel where you had to crouch.

We sat in a line, sipping water, munching on crackers, when a screeching sound filled the tunnels.

"What's that?" Joey asked, clearly terrified.

"One of the tunnel doors opening," I answered, but no one else knew about these tunnels. At least, that was what we thought.

"Some secret these turned out to be," Snow muttered, but I saw his hand go to the gun on his side.

"Just be quiet," Poe whispered.

I feared little Rosie wouldn't be, but she surprised us all with her silence. The sound came again and then nothing.

"Are we sure it was a door?" Simon asked, and I watched with bated breath as Black slowly moved closer to where the sound had come from.

"Where does this door lead?"

"That would be the train station," I said. I was surprised how much my memory kept locked in there about the tunnels. My grandmother had shown me maybe a couple of times at best.

"I suspect it was just a door near this entrance scraping." He pointed down. "I see light from there. The sound must've traveled."

The heaviness in my chest lifted and I breathed a sigh of relief. "We should move, we have a couple of miles yet."

No one complained, not even little Rosie. She and Teddy were whisper singing, and while total silence would have been ideal, the little girl was being so well behaved.

My back, legs, and feet were aching. Several times my knees locked, and I had to stop. I wished I had more time with Elliott, and while I felt amazing most days, I wasn't one hundred percent.

"Here." Black's voice echoed.

"That's it." Poe moved a little to the side to give Black room to work the door. I hoped it didn't make a loud noise or else the whole element of surprise would be ruined.

Fate was on our side, for sure. The slight screech was fast, and we all froze and listened. No sounds came. Black poked his head in the doorway.

"Fuck, that's a lot of stairs."

"The estate is built on a mountain. My great great grandfather had stairs moving around it. Had he done a straight up ladder, then it would've hurt the integrity of the mountain and the foundation." I don't know why I vomited out that information, but I was nervous.

"Whatever. I hope you're all good to handle them."

I knew I wasn't. There was no way I could climb them all as fast as the others.

"Poe."

He turned and I knew when he met my gaze he'd understand.

"I'll carry you."

I chuckled at the grand entrance we'd make with me on his back, and Poe trying to keep me balanced.

"No, let me bring in the rear. You all go, I'll get there eventually."

Poe was about to argue when Jones spoke. "These stairs are wider than I thought. We'll all take turns carrying you and the kids, if we must. We all make it to the top together, we walk in together. And we take down this motherfucking dynasty together."

I hadn't really heard Jones say much until now. He was a man of few words, but when he spoke they were worth the wait.

"Agreed," Christopher said, and soon everyone was in. I felt they'd force carry me if I objected further, so I held my hands up in surrender.

"On my back." Jones crouched down and Poe helped me up. "Whoever carries Phin the longest gets the master bedroom of this castle."

We chuckled, but there was no hiding the fear of the unknown. We didn't know what awaited us at the top, but we'd face it together.

Chapter Thirty-Seven

Poe

Our trek to the top was far harder than the tunnels. We were sweaty, our legs were weak, and the kids had to be just about done with this.

"Okay, stop." Christopher placed Phin down. We were almost to the top and Jones, Black, and Christopher all had carried him. "Remember the plan we discussed last night?" We nodded, but he felt compelled to tell us. "Kids stay here with protection. When it's safe, we'll open the tunnel door and you'll come in. If we don't return, you go back the way we came. Understand?"

It was a gutting realization to think we wouldn't, but we had to be prepared for all scenarios.

"You all have to make it back." Addy's small voice quivered. "We have a Halloween party, you all promised."

We were supposed to do it in the penthouse, but that wasn't going to happen now. She was only eleven and where she was brilliant and at times seemed older than her years, it was moments like this I was reminded of the four-year-old girl I held close to my chest when the lightning was too bright and the thunder too loud.

"We'll have that party," Simon said. "My pops, Snow, all these guys have faced way worse than this and come out on top. You have my word they'll make it out winners." He winked at Christopher who just narrowed his eyes at his nephew.

"Thanks so much for that pressure, Eight," Snow huffed. "Guess we can't die, guys, we wouldn't want to taint Simon's good word."

Unbelievably, we all chuckled. But a second later, it was all business.

"Adelaide, Simon, Joey, Rosie, Sara, and Patricia, you're all staying and with you are Teddy, Ginger, Quill, Angel, and Gina." Angel and Gina were both my security, Ginger had training, Teddy was there to keep the kids calm, and Quill, Sara, and Patricia didn't have experience in these situations at all. Not that Snow or Phin did really, but Snow was adamant, and Phin was an important key.

"When we get up there, Tony, you're in charge of not letting anyone near this tunnel. My guys stay with you," Christopher said, and there was no argument. Those kids were safe inside and outside the tunnel.

We had our orders; we'd enter two by two. Black and Jones first. Followed by Riordan and Lee. With one last look at the kids, Black opened the hidden door. We were met with ghostly silence and stale smells. Black moved to the left of the doorway and Jones to the right. Riordan and Lee followed, and we piled in.

The corridor went both ways, but I knew the kitchens were to the right and staff were our safest bet right now. I gestured that way and in the order we entered the hallway, we vigilantly moved in that direction.

The farther down the corridor we traveled the more sounds we heard. Clanging pots, the whirring of the dishwasher. We were so close to the kitchen. Nostalgia wrapped itself around me as we turned the corner and the kitchen came into view. Finally, the aromas I remembered tickled my nose, and through the archway I saw a much older Jana pass by, pot in hand.

It had been many years since I'd seen the woman who'd kept her mouth shut when Phin and I went to the theater room that day the rest of the world gathered around their televisions to see if they'd found JFK Jr's body. Many years since she would sneak sourdough and jam to me to bring to Phin. Many years since I'd left and she'd promised to stay and watch over him the best she could.

If there was anyone in this house who would help us, it was her.

"Is that Jana?" Phin whispered behind me and I nodded.

"Black." I tilted my head in the direction of the kitchen. "Let me talk to her." He wanted to argue, that was evident in his scowl. "She's not going to interfere, I know it."

"Fine, but any sign she plans to, I'll have to take her out, Poe."

I understood completely. I was going on my gut that Jana stayed behind to protect Phin and stayed after he left just in case he ever returned. I stepped into the kitchen and quickly assessed the room. It was just her and the other door across the way was shut.

"You wouldn't happen to have any sourdough and jam, Jana, would ya?" It was what I always said when I found her in here. Usually she'd chuckle and point to the pantry where she hid it, but this time was different.

She'd been mid-stir when I spoke, now she was stock still. Without turning, she just pointed to the pantry.

"Turn around, Jana, please."

She moved slowly but finally, when she faced me, there was disbelief on her face. Not anger or disappointment; she didn't scream or yell for help. The years were kind to her and while she was probably in her sixties, she didn't look a day over forty. There were more laugh lines than I remembered, her hair had more shades of gray in it.

"Raven?" she whispered and immediately darted for the other door. Black stepped into the room, but I raised a hand to him to wait. Sure enough, she just latched the door to lock it. She turned around with a gasp at the sight of Black in the kitchen, gun in hand.

"He's with me, protection."

She nodded and took a few steps closer to me. "Is it really you?" Her hands cupped my cheeks and tears brimmed her eyes. "I try to keep up on things going on in Haven Hart, loving the glimpses of you in the papers and on TV. You're such a presence. Your parents would be so proud of how you keep things together."

I placed my hands atop hers still cradling my face. "You're aware of who I am then, that I married Phin years ago?"

She chuckled. "Of course. The secrets spoken inside these walls are almost as precious as your coveted vaults."

"I missed you, Jana. And I want so much to talk longer with you, but we came here to find out who's still in the house. So much has happened the last few hours and…"

"I know. I saw the breaking news. The mayor telling everyone the Hart family would be assisting. Of course, I knew that meant you since no one else would be lifting a finger."

"Who's here?"

She released my face and took a step back. "Not many these days. So many fled these last couple of years. Especially when Trenton Hart announced he'd be bringing the Hart name back with a vengeance."

It made sense now why there was so much lacking in the Hart family's schedules. They weren't even here anymore.

"If we were to walk these halls who would we encounter?" Black had put his gun away and softened his stance.

"Well, Trenton has been gone for a few days, but he doesn't usually stay here, he just visits. He has another place in the city. Mallory, her and the kids are never here anymore, either. All that are here are Edward and Mary." They were cousins of Phin's grandmother, both in their eighties.

"If it's just Edward and Mary, why'd you latch the door?" Black asked.

"Because I saw the news, and you showing up here out of the blue after years, I suspected something."

"Someone else is with me, Jana." I walked over to the doorway. Phin was between Frank and Snow. He took my hand and I brought him into the kitchen.

Jana practically fell to her knees when she saw Phin limp into the kitchen. "Sweet heavens, is this real?"

Phin smiled and went to Jana who engulfed him in a motherly embrace. "It's real, Jana."

"I have so many questions," she said through happy laughter.

"And we'll answer all of them, but we need your help, too." Black guided the others into the kitchen. "First, let's make introductions."

Chapter Thirty-Eight

Phin

Jana wouldn't let go of my hand, even when I sat down and rested my legs. At some point I'd developed a limp, and all I could figure was it happened before they carried me up the stairs. I had to remember I was still healing.

Black made introductions and Jana knew quite a few of the people. Christopher and Snow, for sure, but only because of their names being in the paper.

"Without Trenton here, we can secure the estate; however, once it's secure, perhaps we can figure out a way to lure him inside," Black said.

"I'm going to go back toward the tunnels and gather the others. The place is safe and we should put them in an area that can be guarded before we call anyone back in here," Christopher said, and we watched him go flanked by Frank.

"What about the men by the gate?" Snow asked.

"Let's secure inside and then we can open the gates."

I stayed in the kitchen while the others went to secure the estate. I knew this project would take a while. It was a huge property that once upon a time had over fifty Hart family members living there. I was shocked to hear that many had fled and that Edward and Mary were the only two still here.

I never favored either of them, and they had to be pushing ninety by now. With all the Harts gone, Haven Hart was Trenton's playground. He was silently building an army and figuring out how to destroy Poe's power this whole time. He likely wanted to secure it, own it all, and lord it over every living Hart family member and force them to beg for a morsel.

"Can I get you anything?" Jana asked as she began filling two bowls with stew.

"I'm alright for now. When the others get back perhaps we can eat?"

She smiled warmly. "Let me bring Mary and Edward their food, then I'll see what else I have to make."

She left and I was alone. Poe was helping find a safe space for Adelaide and the others. I chuckled when I thought about what Jana would think of her.

This place, once filled with voices and laughter, arguments and hysterics, was beyond quiet. I closed my eyes and remembered the filled kitchen that used to have staff coming in and out. Christmas was perfect madness with too many cookies, ornate decorations, and music filtering through the speakers. Even when I left here, the house still felt alive. It was as if my father died, and the last of any strong Hart family member went with him.

He was a dangerous man and I wouldn't have put it past him to have killed Pricilla to get his hands on Adelaide, but never to hurt her. He'd want to cultivate her. His hatred for Christopher and Black was that of a man vying for power and using sketchy people to obtain it. What my uncle was doing was irreparable. I knew in the end he would die, and me and Adelaide would be it as far as the bloodline left in this city and town. Sure, I could try and find the scattered family, but for what? They didn't support my choices and they never stood up to my father or Trenton.

"Okay, now, let's make dinner." Jana came back into the kitchen and started pulling things out. I smiled as I watched her cook and remembered how she'd tried to teach me every dish, but I told her my expertise was in the tasting.

"So, you had a little girl," Jana said between bites. She made a roasted chicken, three actually since there were so many of us. There were biscuits, vegetables, potatoes. We were ravenous and when we all got to the table, we just said thank you and dove in.

"I'm sorry I was never able to get word to you."

She waved me off. "I understand. Your uncle, he went crazy, Phin."

She didn't need to elaborate. The last week alone proved that to be true.

We spent our meal talking about shifts and how we'd secure the house. Trenton left the estate quite vulnerable, but Jana told us there was no way he ever expected us to come back.

"He had asked that I inform him of any guests or inquiries. I've never given him reason to distrust me and no one ever visits."

Everyone was silent for a fraction of a second, then Jones began laughing, followed by Lee and Black.

"What am I missing?" Their odd humor was addicting, and I found myself smiling.

"I think they discovered exactly how they're going to lure Trenton Hart and his assassins here," Poe answered with a knowing grin. "We can't get comfortable. He could show up at any time, regardless of how often or not he came before. After dinner, let's meet in the study and go over everything." Everyone agreed with him on that.

Jana went with Patricia and Sara after dinner. There was a music room and Adelaide asked if she could play something, and Jana wasn't missing that for anything. Simon offered to take Rosie with him to give Teddy a break and allow him to be in on the meeting. He gladly accepted and Joey followed along.

"We'll need Jana in on this, so after we've planned it all out, I'll have to talk with her, or Phin can." Poe walked toward a large oak armoire. It was filled with old maps, even scrolls.

"More blueprints?" Lee joked.

"Yes, actually. But these are of the estate. Sans the tunnels, of course, since no one knew about them aside from a few, and they made sure to hold the secret close to their vest." Poe slapped a few on the desk. Lee snagged one as did Quill and Snow.

"They are broken down into floors," I said, knowing these maps well. "There's another map in there, newer, about fifteen years old. It's clear. I'm sure there's been renovations and equipment upgrades, but I do remember my father changing some of the structure to add security measures."

Poe found a clear map and unrolled it, showing it was actually several. "Each floor has its own map and own security. Everyone grab a floor and a clear map."

"It's also broken down into wings, Jesus fuck." Quill released a frustrated breath.

"A few times we found people camping out in areas we never visited. My father wanted to secure them, so he thought this was best. If they put them into a computer system, I have no clue about that." I opened my own map, and once we had them all assembled, we began to figure out where we'd all be, and how we'd lure Talos' and Peluda's guys one way, and Trenton the other.

We worked well into the night, and by three a.m., we were all exhausted. Jana showed people where they could sleep while Jones organized shifts to keep an eye out.

I brought Poe to my old bedroom, and he laughed when he saw no one had ever changed a thing. "You had a strange love for Edgar Allan Poe."

I shrugged and pulled him to me. "Only after I met you, and believe it or not, you have some things in common. More so now that you're older."

He smirked and raised a brow in question. "I've read The Raven, Phin. The bird was a symbol for him to represent mournful and never-ending remembrance for his lost love. He spoke to the Raven as a form of catharsis and said Raven, who tries to tell him to give up, she's gone, turns into the embodiment of evil. How am I like that?"

"I meant like Edgar Allan Poe himself. The mystery and macabre." I held up goofy jazz hands and Poe chuckled.

"If you say so. Come. Let's sleep, we need to be up soon, and I have a feeling we have a long day ahead of us."

Sleep came easily to me in the embrace of Poe's arms, and I did in fact dream of a raven with blood red eyes flying over a burning city.

Chapter Thirty-Nine

Poe

The sounds of the house when no one was awake was eerily calming. It brought me back to my childhood when I found solace in the hallways away from the painful light. I had the last shift with Ginger and Snow. We were on separate areas, and it was so spread out I couldn't hear them at all.

It was an hour later when we were all around the dining table eating a hearty breakfast that Black explained to Jana what we required from her. I felt bad asking her to put her life on the line, but it was the only way and she readily agreed.

"When you're all situated, I'll call Trenton; tell him Poe is in the house trying to take over the estate. He'll come and I'll tell him I'm unsure where you went. You think his men will spread out in search of him?"

"It's a gamble, but I do," Black said. "If not we'll have eyes everywhere and we'll figure it out. But I think like Talos and Peluda. I'd spread out to cover more ground as fast as possible."

We all helped Jana clean up and Phin, Christopher, and I followed her into the study to make the call to Trenton. We had her put it on speaker to hear everything.

"Jana? What is it? I'm very busy." His rude tone igniting the simmering anger I woke with.

"I'm so sorry, sir, but you asked me to inform you of any visitors or problems on the estate."

There was a beat of silence before he spoke. "And?"

"Sir, do you remember Raven?" She rolled her eyes as she feigned stupidity.

"Of course I do, Jana, don't ask stupid questions."

"Right, apologies, sir. He's here. He came in and..." This last part we added to entice Trenton himself to come. There was a possibility he'd just send the assassins, but we needed him. This was the guarantee.

"And what, Jana? For Christ sake, spit it out. I'm a busy man!"

"Sir, he brought Phineas Hart with him."

This time the silence was longer. "How? Was he in a bed hooked to things? He's in a vegetative state, Jana." There was no anger in his tone. There was a quiver that spoke to the fact he wasn't one hundred percent sure of Phin's situation.

"He walked right in behind him. I couldn't believe it. Alive and well, I thought..."

Trenton cut her off. "Was there a child?"

We hadn't discussed telling him about Adelaide, so his next words were chilling.

"Was it a girl?"

Phin and I locked eyes. He suspected a girl all the time. I nodded to Jana.

"Yes, sir. The spitting image of Phineas."

"Shit. Her name?"

This time I shook my head. I wasn't giving him more than what he already had.

"I can't remember, I'm sorry."

"Was it Adelaide?"

How would he get that name? There's no way he'd know unless... Unless he knew what Gregor Mims was up to, unless he was behind that, too.

"Sorry, sir. I was too frightened. You must come here. I don't know what to do."

"Very well, I'll be there as soon as I can. Don't let them know I'm coming. Was anyone else with them?"

"No, just them. I did overhear them saying their group had to separate. I don't understand what that means."

Trenton chuckled darkly. "No, you wouldn't. I'll be there soon." The call was cut off, and Jana released a breath and sat back.

"Excellent work, Jana," Christopher said.

"So all this time he knew?" Phin's voice rose.

"Sounds like he suspected, Phin. And it's possible he was working with Gregor Mims and that crazy bitch Vanessa."

"Bryce was hired by an agency to be your assistant. While your art means a lot to you, the business side of it was too much, so you hired him on. But according to what Ginger told us when he was held, it was Vanessa who worked the Poe angle. Lee confirmed Bryce was approached after he worked for Poe. I do agree Gregor and Vanessa were interested in Adelaide, but maybe not for Trenton at the start. Bryce was just a piece of all this, and likely your uncle had his fingers in the pie of it all. That's how it all interconnects." Christopher figured it out. It was so obvious we never suspected it. Trenton just wanted his hands on the girl.

"Do you think he wanted Adelaide and knew nothing about it, and it was through Bryce and Gregor he got pieces of that info?" Phin asked.

"What I think is Gregor wasn't a complete idiot. He wasn't giving Trenton everything until he got paid, and he likely didn't get all his funds. Bryce was able to give Trenton as much info as he could and was paid for that information." I knew this to be true. Bryce was in there because of both Gregor and Trenton. And because I was too busy, I missed it. I had to know exactly what Trenton's involvement was. Before he died, I needed to know that.

"Why you ever thought you could do this on your own is beyond me, Poe," Christopher said. "I get it, I do. It took me a long time to seek help for anything, but you had lives on the line.

You can't ever take this stuff on your shoulders alone again. We'll get out of it, but then we're all in this together until the end. You owe us that, and we owe you to carry some of the burden."

I nodded, at a loss for words on how to respond. I trusted nobody for years to the point I thought I could handle it. In return, I could very well have sentenced us all to death and Haven Hart to ashes.

"You're a God among men," Christopher said. "Your power comes with a price. You, me, Black, we all suffer the same fate." He stepped closer until he was eye to eye with me. "Haven Hart is our Olympus, Poe. Let's do what Gods do and keep it standing."

If it took every drop of blood in my body, I'd save Haven Hart and every person in this house. Trenton wouldn't win.

Forty-five minutes later we were all strategically standing guard in our assigned places. The children, Patricia, and Sara were in a room with only one exit, guarded by Tony, Angel, and Gina. They'd have to get through all of us to make it to that room.

Phin and I were in the study. That was where Trenton would find us, and the others would take out Talos and Peluda silently. The goal was for Trenton to never know his back-up was dead before he was staring down the barrel of a gun assigned to his own death.

Edward and Mary were secure in their room, unaware that any of us were even here. Mary sadly suffered from Alzheimer's and according to Jana, was in the final stages and often had to be sedated. Edward kept to the small garden outside his room and doted on Mary, even though he too was very ill with prostate cancer. Phin was saddened when he heard, but like so many of the Hart family, they didn't stand with him when he tried to fight.

We were still without earpieces, so Lee rigged the gate to

sound when it was opened. The entire house would hear it and everyone would be ready.

It was a little before two when the sound came. Phin gripped my hand as he sat beside me on the sofa in the study.

"I love you, Poe."

"Not more than I love you."

He chuckled. "You and me against the world," he whispered before I felt his lips on mine.

We broke apart a second later. "Always."

Chapter Forty

Phin

So much was lost to me. I had a hard time reconciling my uncle was involved in any human trafficking ring. I heard the story of how Lee, Jones, and Ginger tracked a human trafficking ring in order to save Ginger's brother Joey. How in doing so they discovered Christopher's nephew was a target a while back and Adelaide was, as well. I was curious if Trenton hired someone to find her or got word Gregor had information on her.

"Sir, Sir," Jana's voice echoed in the estate and Poe and I sat behind the closed door of the study, waiting.

"Jana, where are they?"

"After our call ended, there were a couple of security guys who arrived. They went around the estate. But Raven, he's in the study."

That would hopefully make Trenton ask the others he was with to look for the security. And he was certainly predictable.

"Talos, Peluda, search the estate with your men. I can handle Poe on my own. Jana, if I call for you, grab the hunting rifle in the closet by the door. Poe's erratic, he's destroying the city. I'm sure you saw the news?"

"Oh, yes, sir. It's devastating. I'll stand by the study door. If I hear you, I'll come right in."

"You should have one of my men with you." I couldn't tell if it was Talos or Peluda who spoke, but they were probably right.

"I'll be fine. Poe is nothing without his people, plus I have protection on me."

To not give off that we knew Trenton was arriving, we

pretended to be reading something. The click of the study door was loud enough for Trenton to believe we'd hear it.

"Well, well, well," he said as he sauntered in like the king of his domain. "As deep as I've dug, as much information as I've been able to obtain, I missed the fact that my lovely nephew was awake and well."

Trenton's disdained expression was disappointing. If there was any glimmer of hope he'd cared about my well-being at all, it was gone.

"Trenton, isn't this an interesting surprise?" Poe placed the book he was fake reading down. "Have you burned down all the buildings and are also seeking asylum here?"

He chuckled darkly. "This is my asylum, always."

"Tsk, tsk, tsk," Poe said. "No, I'm sorry you don't own this place, so I'll kindly ask you to leave."

Trenton's gaze scanned the room for a moment. He must have been pleased with his assessment because he sat down on the wingback chair across from us, back to the door. So arrogant.

"You and what army, Poe? Your friends have abandoned you. All you have left are a few security guys you hired who are too dumb to realize they lost the war."

Poe just smiled, serene as could be. "Answer something for me, appease a losing soldier, would you?"

Confusion wrinkled Trenton's face for a moment, then he huffed. "What is it?"

"What was your connection with Gregor Mims, Vanessa, and Bryce Evans?"

Trenton's booming laugh was no doubt heard throughout the estate. He found humor in the suffering of children. *Who was this man?*

"It really is the one huge thing I was able to get one up on you." He adjusted his position and it was like he was settling in to tell us a bedtime story. We'd listen because we needed to know, but it also bought the others more time to take out Talos and Peluda's people.

"It's why I must know."

Trenton gave Poe a curt nod. His gaze flickered to me briefly, but it was like I didn't matter. Poe was the player all these years, the one that turned Trenton's world on its side.

"I knew Phineas coupled with Pricilla to make his father happy, and when he left to go to Paris, I was all too pleased to see him go. I felt I could take over after his father died. After all, I tried to get chummy with my nephew in the hopes he'd adore me more than his old man and do my bidding, but that didn't work."

That wasn't the first time I'd heard my uncle's love wasn't true, but it still hurt to hear it. Sometimes I wondered if anyone in this family had loved me growing up aside from my grandmother.

"Then I found out about that child, that one existed. I discovered everything in fragments. First thing was when my brother died, I had to get rid of Phineas, and I hoped I'd legally get the power. But no." Trenton sneered. "You saw to that, Poe, didn't you?"

Poe shrugged. "It wasn't wise to give someone so unstable power. None of you deserved it. I had to secure it."

Trenton huffed. "I began digging and could get nowhere. Who better to find a rich, spoiled child then the sickos who hunt them?"

"You sought out Gregor Mims?" I asked, unable to process much of this. *Why would he do this?*

"I put out feelers and that chick Vanessa got in touch with me. We worked together for a time. I paid her to start looking, and it was she who found Bryce. That shit was able to give us things here and there. I paid him five thousand a month for next to nothing. But then Vanessa mentioned the name Adelaide to me." He rolled his eyes at the name. "Stupid name and I thought it was a destination. She told me it wasn't, and before we stopped talking, I told her if she got the child I'd pay for it."

"And what exactly would you have done with her when you got her?" I asked.

"Use her. Blackmail Poe into giving me what I wanted, and once it was secure, I'd give her back. But things didn't go as planned so…" He held out his arms. "Here we are." Trenton chuckled. "I have to say, Poe, I didn't see all of this coming. You were one hell of an adversary."

"That's the difference between you and me, one of many, actually. You saw this as a game and I saw this as life. It's also why I never gave you more than you had, and why you'll never have Haven Hart." Poe's tone was even, a lingering threat delivered with ice-cold presentation.

"Won't?" Trenton stood and walked over to the drink trolley. "You've lost, Poe. You have nothing left. It took years, but I've beaten you. You're weak and you're using threatening words to make me believe you." I watched as he poured himself two fingers worth of bourbon.

Poe released a low chuckle. It was more telling than anything else and Trenton turned, drink in hand. "Oh, Trenton. You really are a bigger fool then I gave you credit for." He stood and stepped close to Trenton, a little too close for my liking.

Trenton towered over Poe but still, there was a power that clung to him. His presence was fierce, not his size, and Trenton was looking a little confused.

"In the words of Sun Tzu, 'Appear weak when you are strong, and strong when you are weak.'"

"What the hell's that supposed to mean?" Trenton said, just when a thump was heard outside the study.

"Jana," Trenton shouted, but she didn't come.

"I don't think she'll be helping you, Trent." Poe's smile dripped with disdain.

"Talos, Peluda?" He raced to the door, and right when he got there, it opened. Peluda stood there, frozen almost.

"Oh thank God," Trenton laughed. "I thought—"

Just then Peluda dropped to his knees and fell at Trenton's feet. A knife was lodged in his back and blood soaked his shirt.

"You really should read Sun Tzu, Trent. Education is very important," Poe said, but Trenton didn't move, not at first.

Ever so slowly, I saw Trenton reach into his jacket. And the shine of a handgun glinted off of the lighting.

"Poe, gun!" I yelled and rushed my uncle. I wasn't strong enough to fight him, but he dropped the gun and we both fell atop Peluda's lifeless body.

"Phin!" Poe shouted, and suddenly I was lifted off Trenton and thrown against the couch. I looked up in time to see Black and Christopher there. Poe had one of Trenton's arms pinned. Two guns were trained on Trenton and I breathed in relief.

"Game over, Trent, you lose." Poe gritted his teeth, and then it all happened so fast.

Poe turned his head toward me and smiled. A victory, it was over. It was in his expression. Pure and utter joy. But movement caught my eye. Peluda was still next to them as they were spread on the floor, and Trenton grabbed the knife. I screamed at the same moment Trenton pulled it from Peluda's back, and lunged it into Poe's chest. It happened in a matter of seconds, and the same moment Trenton stabbed Poe, Black and Christopher shot Trenton. But the damage was done.

Poe fell backward, the knife securely impaled in his chest.

"Phin," he whispered, before his head fell backward.

"No!" I shouted and went to him. "Poe! No!"

But he didn't move, not even a flicker.

Chapter Forty-One

Phin

"I think if I never met you, I'd always feel like I was missing something, does that make sense?"

Poe chuckled as he gripped my hand. He was leaving tomorrow per my father's instructions, so we were hanging out in the treehouse. The stars were spectators to our farewell.

"When I'm not near you, it feels like I'm unplugged." *He turned and pressed his body against mine.* *"We're stronger than anyone knows, Phin. You have to always believe that, never forget it, and one day, you and I will be together, and no one will stand between that."*

I could see how much he believed that as he hovered over me, gaze roaming my face. If I never saw him after tonight, I'd never love again. I may only be sixteen, but I knew Poe was my forever and a day.

"I like the pictures you paint of us, Poe."

He glided his hand up my stomach and stopped over where my heart beat. *"Art is real life frozen in time, Phin. When you feel like everything is moving around you too fast, close your eyes and paint a picture of us. I'll make it real, I promise."*

I knew Poe would move heaven and earth to make my dreams come true. I knew it the day he smiled at me for the first time. When he kissed me awkwardly, and we spent hours perfecting it. I knew it when he brought me sourdough and jam, and when he looked at me.

"I promise to paint the best pictures ever."

"Phin!"

I turned at the sound of my name. Snow was running toward me. I didn't care about explanations or anything. I called for an ambulance, asked Jana to stay with Adelaide, hopped in with Poe, and stood in the emergency room alone for what felt like hours.

"Phin, how is he? What's happening?" Snow's eyes scanned the whole area like something would jump out and hurt us. Was this our life now? Unable to know if the threats were really gone?

"He... I don't know."

With a force I wasn't expecting from such a small man, he grabbed my arm and pulled me to him in a strong embrace.

"He is Poe. Even death fears him." He pulled back and his piercing blue eyes held me prisoner. "He fought for you and Adelaide. He went head to head with monsters scarier than Trenton Hart. He did it alone when he had to, burned bridges he likely needed, he's not dying today, Phin." He pointed a pale finger at my chest. "No way he's missing out on loving you forever."

I wanted Snow's prophecy to be real. My legs gave out in that moment, but I never fell. Snow gripped my arms and helped me to one of the chairs. I wept like I never did before. This hurt more than when I lost my grandmother. More than discovering my entire family would sooner piss on my ashes than love me. I couldn't lose him, not when we finally had a chance to be together.

Snow talked as I sobbed in his shoulder. He rubbed my back and shoulders, told me how some woman named Maggie was complaining about all the glass she had to clean up after Peluda's men broke in. Then he shared with me about how she liked arguing with him. I knew he was just doing it to keep my mind off things.

At some point I sat up, rubbed my eyes, and took in the room. Everyone was there, how'd I miss their arrival? Black and Quill sat on some chairs, eyes glued to the television that was reporting the chaos in Haven Hart. Christopher was on his phone talking to someone about Talos and Peluda. I heard him whisper their names. I knew they were dead, and I knew it was quick, painless, and discrete. Ginger, Jones, and Lee were huddled in a circle talking; again, I only heard pieces of it. Lee was telling Ginger that Menagerie was cleared of the hit the second he put the word out that Trenton Hart was dead. Teddy had Rosie on his lap, and Riordan was showing Joey and Simon something on some device.

Adelaide was fast asleep against Patricia. Sara, Tony, and the others were all in similar states in the waiting room chairs. The room was filled. None of us wondering what tomorrow would bring, just that we made it. We survived… I hoped we all did.

"Excuse me?" I looked up and saw a nurse. "Are you all family of a Raven Edgars?" In unison they all said yes, and if I wasn't eager for a report on him, I'd be struck to tears by the unity.

"I'm looking for his husband."

I stood on shaky legs, grateful when everyone seemed to gather around me, whether to physically or emotionally support me, I wasn't sure.

"I'm his husband, I'm Mr…"

"Edgars?" the nurse said, and I realized I wanted that. I didn't want to answer any hard questions about my name.

"Yes, I'm Mr. Edgars. How is he? How's my husband?"

She gestured for me to follow and I realized everyone was joining me. "You maybe should stay here, guys. There's too many of us and I don't want to scare anyone."

"I'm going with you," Snow said, gripping my hand and leading me over to where the nurse, and now a doctor I'd know anywhere, stood.

"Ah, Mr. Edgars, I'm Doctor Bailey." He winked at me so only Snow and I could see. This was the man who came to my house almost every day for three years to take care of me. He wasn't there the day of the attack, and I was so glad he was okay, and shocked to see him here.

"Doctor Bailey." I held out my hand.

He asked the nurse to excuse us, and when she was out of earshot, he spoke. "He's okay, Phin. It was touch and go for a while, I won't lie. He flat-lined three times, but, he's strong."

I had to lean against the nurse's station as relief washed over me. "Can I see him?"

"You need to hear me, Phin." He waited until he had my undivided attention. "He lost a lot of blood. The knife missed his heart by inches. I'm grateful in times like this that people think the heart is directly in the center of the chest, but there are still so many areas that if punctured could be fatal. He was lucky."

"Will he recover?" Snow asked.

"I think he will, but I say that because I've seen miracles in you, Phin."

"I need to see him."

Doctor Bailey nodded. "Okay, he's in recovery after surgery. I'll come get you when he's in ICU."

"I'll let everyone know," Snow said and slipped away.

"Phin." Doctor Bailey stepped closer. "I'm so glad to see you're okay. You and Poe and your little girl have a lifetime to finally live. Enjoy every second." He patted my shoulder and walked away.

As I stood there watching Doctor Bailey retreat, I thanked whoever was listening. Maybe it was my grandmother who made sure we got out of this. I didn't know, I just knew I was eternally grateful.

By the time I made it to the ICU, a numbing calm came over me. I knew Poe was going to live, and we were going to have years together. It wasn't all for nothing, it was everything for a forever.

I kissed his cheek and sat beside him like he did for me all those years. I shared with him all that happened and how Corey said he'd come by to drive him home when he was better. I talked and talked and talked. Even when he opened his gorgeous dark eyes, I kept on talking. I held his hand and never let go.

Chapter Forty-Two

Poe
One Month Later

"Happy Halloween!" Adelaide shouted when Quill, Black, and Joey entered the house. It wasn't really Halloween, we missed it by about three weeks, but she was promised a Halloween party so, we made sure it happened.

When Trenton Hart plunged that knife into my chest, I felt no pain. I remember thinking at least Phin's okay. Adelaide will be safe. Life didn't flash before my eyes; fear didn't try and suffocate me. I knew that if my life ended then, it would be okay because everyone I loved was alive.

"Well, look at you," Quill said in his Flash costume. "Are you a princess unicorn cat... I'm sorry, I'm not experienced in little girl, what are you?"

I chuckled at Quill's obvious awkwardness.

"I'm Countess Cocoa Puff's Fairy Godicorn," Adelaide said with a roll of her eyes.

"Yeah, Quill, duh." Black rolled his eyes in imitation and leaned down to hug Adelaide. "You look gorgeous."

"Who are you?" I took in Black's hairy outfit but was at a loss.

"King Kong of course."

Joey wore a simple zombie outfit and shrugged as he walked in behind them. He really had become a permanent fixture at Black and Quill's, and Ginger told me his and Joey's relationship was better than ever.

"How're you feeling?" Christopher came up behind me dressed as Mr. Incredible. He looked amazing in the unitard.

"Better, tired, and Phin won't let me do anything."

I was in a coma for a week, and while I believed Phin when he said he heard things and felt people, I experienced none of that. I remembered waking and seeing his tear stained face, kissing his chapped lips, and reveling in his scent. He was safe and I was alive.

"Take it easy. Black is rebuilding his tower of murder in a few months, and he has ideas for all of us apparently." Snow laughed. He was Elastigirl and Simon was Dash. They were ridiculous and I loved it.

"Oh? I can't wait to hear those ideas." My voice dripped with sarcasm.

The last month was a clusterfuck. Police, FBI, every law enforcement agency, descended on Haven Hart. In the end, we couldn't get away from tainting the Hart name. Trenton Hart's name to be more precise. Lee worked his magic and created a trail of greed, power, and jealousy right to Trenton's doorstep.

When asked why Kingpin Christopher Manos and Terrance Blackrose were at the Hart estate the evening Trenton Hart was killed, that was where we had to get creative. Tony, my head of security, said the three were having a meeting after the building collapsed, and while unlikely allies, we wanted to make the city strong for all our sakes. Trenton Hart arrived enraged and tried to shoot us after he vowed to stop whatever we had planned. Tony told authorities how Trenton gloated at his ability to dismantle the Blackrose Tower, and he'd continue his destruction until Haven Hart was the mecca he envisioned. In defense, he was shot from legally owned guns, but before he died, he stabbed me. Now, I wouldn't say the authorities believed it all, but in the end, they couldn't prove otherwise.

"Since we can't go trick or treating, we have a ton of games planned." Phin came to my side and wrapped his arm around my waist. He wore a Superman costume and I was Lex Luther. Surprisingly, I had "evil chic" clothes, as Phin put it.

"Can't wait." Simon smiled and went over to where the other kids were.

"When you have a moment, Christopher and Snow, will you join Phin and me in our study? I just need to gather a few others, but I need to talk to you all."

They agreed and Phin went to gather everyone. I walked down the hall to the study. The house was set back to rights a couple of weeks after the ambush. We came back because this was our home, and Haven Hart was still in a bit of a mess. We weren't sure we'd move closer, but we knew we'd be going into Haven Hart a lot. The estate wasn't ours. We hadn't felt the connection to it that others may have. Jana remained there most of the time to keep it going and allow Edward and Mary a place to live until their passing.

One night, as we were in bed, Phin said he thought maybe he'd make the estate a museum. Allow people to tour it and enrich their lives with the many amazing things his grandmother would want people to know about Haven Hart.

I told him once I was up and moving, we'd make sure to get the ball rolling on that. Jana would love to have a bustling house again.

I sat in one of the chairs and waited until everyone arrived. Slowly they did. Teddy and Riordan were first, followed shortly by Christopher and Snow. Phin arrived with the rest. Lee, Ginger, Jones, Mace, Bill, Black, and Quill.

"What's going on? We're missing the Monster Mash," Ginger said. I smiled at his Deadpool costume, and the fact he'd convinced Jones and Lee to dress up was hilarious. Lee was The Riddler, Jones was Bane.

"I won't take up a lot of your time, I promise." I opened the drawer beside me and took something out. When I placed them on the table in front of me, Snow gasped.

"The keys."

"I made you all a promise when this was over there'd be no more secrets between us. It all remains the same that if Phin and I both die, all of you get what we discussed. But in the meantime." I pushed the keys farther to the center.

"I realize now I can't do this alone. I can't keep Haven Hart safe from all who want to destroy it. The secrets were killing me and I am asking for help."

Everyone was silent and then Teddy stepped forward and picked up the keys.

"Wait, these are it? These are what keep the vaults locked?" He looked at all of us in disbelief. "This is sort of stupid. I mean, I lose my keys all the time. Are you saying anyone could have snatched these up?"

"No, Teddy, they're ornamental," Riordan answered with an indulgent smile.

"So this was for dramatic effect?" He jangled the keys in front of me.

"You're killing this moment, Teddy," Mace said as he took the keys and tossed them to Phin who caught them.

"Next week, each of you will be given access to all the vaults in Haven Hart." Phin handed me the keys. "Yes, it was for dramatic effect." Everyone chuckled.

"We're going to do this together?" Bill asked. "I mean, can we actually all work together to keep this city up and not kill each other?"

"So negative." Mace tsked. "I have confidence in us."

"I think we can, and when my company is rebuilt, we can use it as a hub. I have plans," Black said.

"But we have to agree."

"Are we working on a voting system?"

"Is there a dress code?"

"There aren't stock options, are there?"

"If we disagree, are you going to put a hit on us?"

Everyone was talking at once and I started laughing. We were a mess, there was no question, but we'd make it work. I believed that. Black and Menagerie were the only large assassin organizations out there, and Menagerie wasn't coming near us. Christopher had his side of things, and we all just knew what we were doing. But when you put all of us in a room, there was bound to be clashing. I looked forward to many years of clashing.

Epilogue

Simon/Eight
FIVE YEARS LATER

I'd just lifted the final thing I needed to pack before leaving in the morning when something caught my eye. It was peeking out from under the suitcase. I tossed the book I'd picked up into the case and gently pried whatever was stuck out from under it.

I'd held it last night as I slept in my childhood bed for the last time. It was a picture taken over the summer for my high school graduation party. Pops had the biggest tent I'd ever seen set up, a live band, food, drinks. Everyone was there.

Teddy had wanted a picture of all of us since it was rare we were all together in the same place. Poe and Phin lived hours away with Adelaide, so we rarely saw them. They'd enjoyed not having to hide anymore, and with the help of Pops, Black, and the others, Haven Hart was deemed one of the safest places to live last year. I allowed myself a few minutes to remember that perfect summer day.

"Can I have everyone's attention, please." Pops was standing on a lawn chair, champagne flute in hand. "There are a couple of servers coming around with champagne, if you could all grab a drink so we can properly toast the graduate."

I chuckled and observed as the servers passed champagne to everyone. Riordan was holding one for him and Teddy as their daughter Rosie did cartwheels around them. Their other daughter, Kerry, was only six months old and currently fast asleep in

Teddy's arms. Their life hadn't changed much over the years. Riordan was still running his security business, and Teddy was still hugging people and kicking ass playing video games.

A loud, boisterous laugh caught my attention. Black was laughing at Quill who was trying desperately to get their three boys to sit still for a minute so they could listen to the toast. Their three boys were holy terrors, and it was easy to see that Quill was the fun parent because a second later Black told the boys to settle and they listened. His tower was rebuilt and better than ever. Lee and Jones were still there and Ginger worked in a much calmer capacity. Black and Quill spent a lot of time here talking long into the night with Pops and Snow. Haven Hart was thriving and they wanted to keep it that way.

Poe, Phin, and Adelaide sidled up next to Black, taking their own champagne and chuckled at the way Black got his sons in order. Phin had become one hell of an athlete over the years. He took part in marathons and triathlons and stopped hiding. He was the face of the Hart family; a kinder, more understanding face, and with Poe and Addy at his side, they'd been the Harts this town had always needed.

Mace and Bill were standing on each side of Pops, and I could tell Bill wasn't convinced the lawn chair would hold him. Typical Bill. He and Mace still lived in the house on the property, but it was just them, no kids, and they loved it that way.

Lee, Jones, and Ginger, along with Ginger's brother Joey and his girlfriend Deena, were all at a table with Snow. Joey never did move in with his brother. He stayed with Black and Quill and because of that, it saved Ginger and Joey's relationship. The throuple still lived in Jones' house off the grid, and all still worked for Black in some way. It was great to see the three of them smiling more.

This was my crazy family, the ones that, after summer ended, I'd drive away from to grow as a person and find myself.

"Simon, I love you. You couldn't make me prouder if you tried. Haven Hart will miss the never ending light you shine on it every day, but I know you'll become something great. And hopefully, whatever path you take, it will lead you back home." Pops lifted his flute and everyone laughed and cheered. It was the perfect summer day.

"Okay!" Teddy shouted. "It's a rare occurrence we're all together, so let's get a picture." We all gathered where he told us, and Maggie took the perfect moment and froze it in time.

"Knock knock." Snow's voice pulled me away from the picture, and I turned to see him leaning against the door frame, eyes glued to my suitcase. "All packed?"

I wanted to speak, but my throat felt clogged, like I'd say something and start crying. I opted for a nod.

"Chris said we'd go after lunch. It's a five flippin hour drive, but we want you to have a full stomach and, well, after lunch, okay?" I saw his blue eyes glistening and knew he was barely holding it together. Snow had been essential in my upbringing. He wasn't biologically mine, but he was in all the ways that mattered.

"You know," I said, trying to find some levity. "I was thinking of bringing my Captain America poster with me." I chuckled when his eyes widened.

"You better or I'll burn it, Iron Man forever!" He held his fist up the same way I did ten years ago in the police station. He rescued me that day and every day thereafter. I'd miss him and Pops so much.

"Captain America is on the right side of justice." I walked over to him, I was eighteen, and had a good foot on him now. He had to crane his head up to look at me.

"Oh, please, in the end it's all the same." His voice cracked on the last word, and without thinking, I wrapped my arms around him.

"I love you, Snow."

"Shut up." His voice was muffled as he pressed against my chest.

"You don't mean that."

He pushed away and his red-rimmed gaze almost broke my heart. "Why couldn't you go to Haven Hart College?"

We'd had this conversation, and I'd honestly thought about it, but in Haven Hart I was Simon Manos, nephew to Christopher Manos. No one ever charged me for coffee, food, even clothes. I wanted to be a regular person who paid for things and wasn't let off the hook because of who I was. I chose a college five hours away where I could figure out who the hell I was.

"Snow, you know why." He was about to say something snarky, I was sure, but I cut him off. "It's going to be fine. It's only five hours from here, and you know if you wanted to see me Pops would fly you to wherever I was and land his helicopter in the middle of the college green."

Snow chuckled and wiped away a stray tear. "He would."

"You'll barely miss me, Snow. I mean you, Teddy, Quill, Xander, Phin, Poe, you're all always busy with your meditation and all their millions of kids." It was true, they all kept themselves plenty busy and Snow loved it.

"Think I can convince Chris to get me a baby?"

I burst out laughing. "He'd get you anything you'd ask for because you never ask for anything but, Snow, you don't get a baby. It's not a dog."

Snow rolled his eyes. "Yeah, yeah."

I turned and zipped up my luggage, slipped in the photo of all twenty whatever of us and hefted it off the bed.

"You promise you'll call at least fifty times a week?" Snow said, earning another chuckle.

"How about once a day?"

"Once?" Snow shouted.

"Yes, I have class."

Snow smiled and shot me a wink. "I have class too, Eight."

I laughed once more and made to leave the room, but he stopped me.

"Promise, Eight. Promise you'll call and not forget us and you'll be safe."

"I promise."

He lifted his hand and I looked at it. He had a pinky raised.

"You have to pinky promise," he said, and once again, I was thrust back to the time I made Snow pinky promise me.

"Okay, Snow." We linked fingers and he gripped mine almost painfully, his blue eyes pierced me.

"You can't ever break a pinky promise. Chris says if you break a promise that's sealed with the hug of a pinky…"

I said the last part with him, "Santa will find out and you'll get no presents."

His smile was sad and my heart ached. Growing up was hard to do, but I knew we'd all be okay.

"Okay, Eight." He released our pinkies but held out his hand. "Let's go to lunch."

And like that night ten years ago, I took Snow's hand and let him lead me to my next adventure.

The End

Other Books by the Author

Haven Hart Series:

Snow Falling

Hug It Out

A Dangerous Dance

From These Ashes

Snow Storm

Triple Threat

Co-written with JM Dabney

The Hunt

Author's Note

Thank you so much for reading Raven's Hart, the final installment in the Haven Hart series. I hope you've enjoyed reading Poe's story and taking this amazing journey with our people of Haven Hart. Please feel free to leave a review, that's always appreciated. I love talking to my readers so you can email me at davidsonkingauthor@yahoo.com or visit my website to chat www.davidsonking.com. I'm also on Facebook and mostly in my reader's group www.facebook.com/groups/davidsonkingscourt.

Acknowledgements

The last acknowledgement in this series… This is difficult. So many people made this possible.

My Beta's: Jenn, Annabella, Luna you've been there from the beginning. Dana, you helped me with Snow Storm and I thank you, Morningstar you got me off to the right start with Snow Falling. Melissa, you were amazing and so helpful during all this.

Thank you to Heidi for pushing me with this series and making me a better writer.

Thank you to Steph for not only perfecting my books but being a shoulder to freak out on.

Thank you Anita for working tirelessly and for your infinite patience.

Jami, oh Jami, my partner in crime and the one who actually will tell me to snap out of it.

Jackie, you're my place to rest. My person where I can just be me and you help me escape my books.

Thank you to Morningstar for her graphics through this WHOLE thing and making one cover better than the next.

To my husband and family. You're saints you put up with my panic attacks, and you let me soundboard off you. You hug me when I need it and love me when I require it. You're everything.

And to ALL my readers, you're my everything. YOU made Haven Hart come to life with your encouragement, love, and support. Thank you.

About the Author

Davidson King, always had a hope that someday her daydreams would become real-life stories. As a child, you would often find her in her own world, thinking up the most insane situations. It may have taken her awhile, but she made her dream come true with her first published work, Snow Falling.

When she's not writing you can find her blogging away on Diverse Reader, her review and promotional site. She managed to wrangle herself a husband who matched her crazy and they hatched three wonderful children.

If you were to ask her what gave her the courage to finally publish, she'd tell you it was her amazing family and friends. Support is vital in all things and when you're afraid of your dreams, it will be your cheering section that will lift you up.

Link to all Davidson's social media and website:
   linktr.ee/davidsonkingauthor

Printed in Great Britain
by Amazon